This book belongs to

_____

My Treasury of ANIMAL Tales & Rhymes

Published by Hinkler Books Pty Ltd
45–55 Fairchild Street
Heatherton Victoria 3202 Australia
www.hinkler.com.au

hinkler

© Hinkler Books Pty Ltd 2012
Content originally appeared in My Nursery Rhyme Collection (© 2006 Hinkler
Books Pty Ltd),
My Treasury of Five-Minute Tales (© 2010 Hinkler Books Pty Ltd),
My Treasury of Bedtime Tales (© 2008 Hinkler Books Pty Ltd),
My Treasury of Fairytales (© 2009 Hinkler Books Pty Ltd)

Cover design: Anton Petrov
Illustrators: Andrew Hopgood, Melissa Webb, Gerad Taylor, Geoff Cook, Bill
Wood, Anton Petrov and Marten Coombe (My Nursery Rhyme Collection);
Brijbasi Art Press Ltd (My Treasury of Five-Minute Tales); Melissa Webb, Anton
Petrov, Omar Aranda, Suzie Byrne, Mirela Tufan and Dean Jones (My Treasury
of Bedtime Tales); Omar Aranda, Suzie Byrne, Melissa Webb (My Treasury of
Fairytales)
Prepress: Graphic Print Group

ISBN: 978 1 7430 8399 4

Printed and bound in China

Contents

Introduction

Sharing fairytales and nursery rhymes with children opens up doors to a world of wonder and mystery and helps foster a love of reading. Not only do fairytales and nursery rhymes engage the imagination of even the youngest children, but they also help to gain an understanding of different situations and emotions.

Animals have appeared in stories and rhymes going back to ancient times and may feature in several ways: the main protagonist who drives the story (The Little Red Hen and The Ugly Duckling); a helper who advises the main character (Puss in Boots); or a threatening figure seeking to take advantage (the wolf in The Three Little Pigs). Animals will often be used to represent aspects of human life and behaviour, a process called *anthropomorphism* (think of a stubborn donkey, a cheeky monkey or a proud peacock).

Nursery rhymes are the beginning of language and are meant to be read aloud – loudly and enthusiastically! It is great fun to make all the animal noises for Old McDonald Had a Farm and to giggle at the Three Little Monkeys jumping on their bed.

The tradition of fairytales and folklore is one that has been with us for centuries. Fairytales are found in every culture and are an important inheritance of a rich oral folktale history that has been developed throughout the ages.

This collection brings together traditional nursery rhymes and classic animal tales from well-known authors such as Hans Christian Andersen, Charles Perrault and the Brothers Grimm.

We hope you enjoy sharing these tales and rhymes.

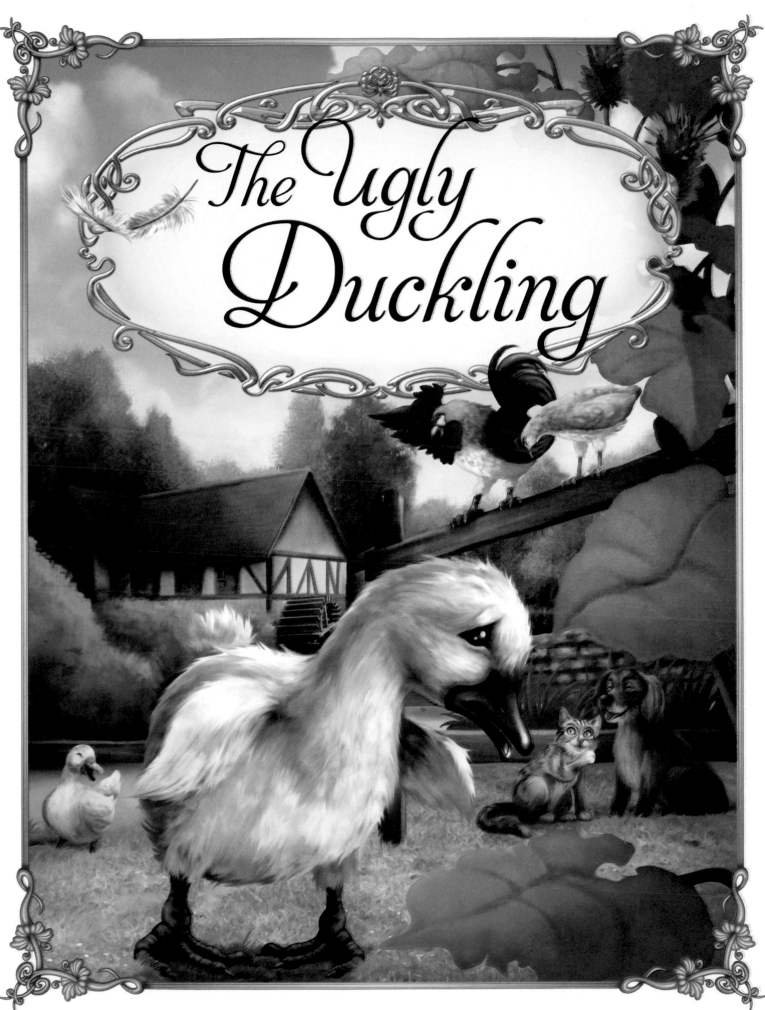

The Ugly Duckling

It was a beautiful summer in the countryside. The corn was golden, the oats were green and the haystacks were piled up in the meadows. The stork walked about on his long red legs chattering away in Egyptian, which his mother had taught him. Surrounding the cornfields and meadows were large forests, in the midst of which were deep lakes. It was indeed lovely.

In a sunny spot near a deep river stood a pleasant old farmhouse. Along the river grew great burdock leaves, so tall that a child could stand underneath them.

In this snug spot, a duck sat on her nest, waiting for her eggs to hatch. She was beginning to get tired of waiting, as her little ones were a long time coming out of their shells and she didn't get many visitors. The other ducks much preferred to swim in the cool river than to climb the muddy slope and gossip with her.

At last, the egg shells cracked, one after the other. From each egg came a little creature that raised its head and cried out, 'Peep, peep!'

'Quack, quack,' said the mother, and then they all quacked as well as they could and looked about them at the large green leaves. Their mother let them look as much as they liked, for green is good for the eyes.

'Are you all hatched?' asked the duck. 'No, I do declare, the biggest egg is still here. I hope this doesn't last too long, as I am quite tired of it.' She settled herself back down on the nest.

An old duck came to visit. 'How are you getting on?' she asked.

'One egg is still not hatched,' replied the duck. 'But the others are the prettiest ducklings you'll ever see!'

The old duck looked at the large unhatched egg. 'I am sure that is a turkey's egg. I was tricked into hatching some once. After all my trouble, they were afraid to go into the water. Take my advice. Leave it where it is and teach the other children to swim.'

'I will sit on it for a little longer,' said the duck. 'A few days longer will be nothing.'

'As you wish,' said the old duck, and she took her leave.

At last, the large egg hatched. A young bird crept out, crying 'Peep, peep!' It was very large and ugly with grey feathers. The duck exclaimed, 'It is so large and not at all like the others! Maybe it really is a turkey. I'll find out when we go to the water. It will go in, even if I have to push it in.'

The next day, the sun shone brightly on the green burdock leaves, so the mother duck took her children down to the water. She jumped in and cried 'Quack, quack!' One after the other, the ducklings tumbled in after her. The water closed over their heads but they all popped up in an instant and were soon swimming about prettily with their legs paddling away underneath them. The ugly duckling was also in the water, swimming as well as any of them.

'Well, he is not a turkey,' said the mother. 'See how well he paddles and how he holds himself upright. He is not so ugly if you look at him properly. Come now children, I will take you into society and introduce you to the farmyard. Stay close to me so you are not stepped on, and, above all, look out for the cat!'

When they reached the farmyard, the mother duck said, 'Let me see how well you can behave. Bow your heads to that old duck there. She is the highest born of them all. See how she has a red flag tied to her leg? It is a great honour and shows that everyone is anxious not to lose her. Come now, bend your neck and say "quack".'

The ducklings did as they were told, but the other ducks stared and said, 'What a queer-looking duckling one of them is!' One spiteful duck flew at the ugly duckling and bit him.

'Leave him alone!' cried his mother. 'He is not doing any harm.'

'He is so big and ugly,' said the nasty duck, 'and he should be turned away.'

'The others are very pretty,' said the old duck. 'What a shame this one cannot be hatched again!'

'He is not very pretty, your ladyship,' said the mother duck, 'but he has a very good disposition and swims better than the others. I think he has just stayed in the egg too long and his figure is not properly formed.'

'The other ducklings are graceful enough,' said the old duck. 'Now make yourself at home.'

The family made themselves at home. But the ugly duckling was chased and pushed and bitten and jeered at by all the poultry in the farmyard. It grew worse every day. The poor duckling was hunted by everyone and even his brothers and sisters taunted him and his mother said she wished he had never been born. At last, he ran away, frightening the little birds in the hedge as he flew over.

'They are afraid because I am so ugly,' the ugly duckling thought. He closed his eyes and flew until he came to a large moor where some wild ducks lived. Here he stayed the night, very tired and sorrowful.

In the morning, the wild ducks stared at him. 'What sort of duck are you?' they asked, crowding around. The duckling bowed to them but he didn't answer.

'You are very ugly,' the wild ducks said, 'but you seem nice and you can stay as long as you don't want to marry any of us.' Poor duckling! All he wanted was to lie among the rushes and drink some water.

He had been there two days when two young wild geese, or rather goslings, came to him. 'You are so ugly that we like you well,' one said. 'Will you travel with us?'

'Pop, pop!' suddenly sounded in the air, and the two geese fell down dead. 'Pop, pop' echoed out and the ducks and geese rose up into the air. Hunters had surrounded the moor and the sound continued from every direction. Then the hunting dogs came running through the rushes.

The poor duckling was terrified! A large, terrible dog came bounding past him with its jaws wide open and its tongue hanging out. It sniffed at the ugly duckling and bared its teeth and its wild eyes gleamed, and then it splashed away without touching him. 'I am so ugly that not even a dog would bite me,' sighed the duckling.

All day he lay still while the guns boomed overhead. It wasn't until late in the day that it became quiet, but the ugly duckling was too scared to move for several hours. He ran away from the moor as fast as he could until a storm blew up.

As night fell, he came to a poor little cottage. The storm was so wild that the duckling could struggle on no further and he sat down beside it. He noticed that one of the door's hinges had given out and the door slanted in such a way that he could sneak inside, which, very quietly, he did.

An old woman lived in the cottage with her tom cat and her prize hen. In the morning, they discovered their guest and the cat began to purr and the hen clucked. 'What is all the noise about?' asked the old woman.

Her eyesight was not very good, so when the old woman saw the duckling, she thought it must be a duck. 'What luck!' she exclaimed. 'Now we shall have duck eggs, unless it is a drake. I'll wait and see.'

The tom cat and the hen thought themselves the master and mistress of the house, and they were not pleased at all. The duckling was allowed to remain in the house on trial, but there were no eggs.

'Can you lay eggs?' the hen asked the duckling.

'No,' he replied.

'Then hold your tongue!' said the hen.

'Can you arch your back, or purr, or hiss?' asked the cat.

'No,' replied the duckling.

'Then stay quiet when sensible people are talking!' said the cat.

The duckling stayed in the corner, feeling very low and sad. Then one day the sunshine and fresh air came into the room through the open door. The duckling was seized with such a longing to go swimming that he could not help but tell the hen about it.

'What is this nonsense?' cried the hen. 'You have nothing to do, so you are filling your head with fancies. If you could lay eggs or purr, you wouldn't have these ideas.'

'But it is so delightful to swim on the water,' said the duckling, 'and so refreshing to dive down to the bottom.'

'Why, you must be crazy!' said the hen. 'Ask the cat if he would like to swim about on the water. Ask our mistress if she would like to dive down and let the water close over her head! I advise you to learn to purr and lay eggs as soon as possible.'

'You don't understand me,' said the duckling. 'I think I must go out into the world again.'

'Indeed you must,' said the hen, and so the ugly duckling left the cottage. Soon he found some water to swim and dive in, but the other animals avoided him because he was so ugly. Autumn came and the leaves turned gold. As winter approached, the trees grew bare and heavy dark clouds hung in the sky.

One evening, as the sun was setting, a large flock of beautiful birds flew overhead. The duckling had never seen any creatures like them before. They were swans, with dazzling white feathers and long, graceful necks, who were flying to warmer countries. They uttered a peculiar cry as they flew.

The ugly duckling felt quite strange as he watched them. He whirled around in the water and, stretching out his neck towards them, he uttered a cry so strange that it frightened him. He was beside himself with excitement and knew that he would never forget those beautiful, proud birds. He felt towards them as he had never felt towards any other creature.

As winter closed in, the weather grew colder and colder. The ugly duckling had to swim about on the water to stop it from freezing, but every morning the space he had left to swim in grew smaller and smaller.

Finally, the water began to freeze around him and he had to paddle with his legs as hard as he could to stop the space from closing completely. He grew so exhausted that he lay still and helpless, frozen in the ice.

The next morning, a farmer was passing by when he found the duckling. He broke the ice around the duckling with his shoe and carried him home to his wife.

The farmer's wife revived the poor creature and then the farmer's children tried to play with him. Not understanding, the duckling thought they wanted to harm him. In his terror, he fluttered into the milk pan and splashed milk about the room. Then he flew into the butter tub and into the meal barrel and out again. What a state he was in!

The woman yelled and chased him with her broom while the children laughed and screamed and fell over each other as they tried to catch him. At last, he slipped out through the open door and lay down exhausted under a bush in the snow.

The poor duckling endured many miseries and privations during the hard winter. He was surviving out on a moor when the sun began to shine and the birds began to sing again for spring.

The duckling found that his wings were stronger and he rose up into the air. He flew until he found himself in a large garden. The trees were in blossom and a stream wound its way through the grounds. Then the duckling saw three beautiful white swans swimming lightly over the smooth water. He remembered these beautiful birds and felt more unhappy than ever.

'I will go to these birds,' he thought. 'Even if they kill me because I am so ugly and I dare to approach them, it would be better than being pecked by the ducks, beaten by the hens or starving of hunger in the winter.'

The duckling landed on the water and swam towards the swans. When they saw him, they rushed to him with wings outstretched.

'Kill me,' said the poor duckling, and he bowed his head down and waited for them to strike him.

But what did he see reflected in the clear stream? He saw his own image; no longer an ugly, grey duckling but a beautiful, graceful young swan. To be born in a duck's nest is of no consequence if one is born a swan. The duckling felt glad to have suffered all the sorrow and hardship, for he was better able to enjoy the pleasure and happiness he now felt. The other swans swam around him and welcomed him.

Some young children came into the garden and threw some bread into the water. 'There is a new one!' they cried. They ran to their mother and father, shouting, 'There is a new swan arrived! He is the most beautiful of all! He is so young and pretty!' And the older swans bowed their heads to him.

Then he felt ashamed and hid his head under his wing, for he did not know what to do. He was so happy, but he was not at all proud. He had been hated for his ugliness and now he heard them saying he was the most beautiful. The sun shone warm and bright and he lifted his head and cried out joyfully, from the bottom of his heart, 'I never dreamed of such happiness as this, when I was an ugly duckling!'

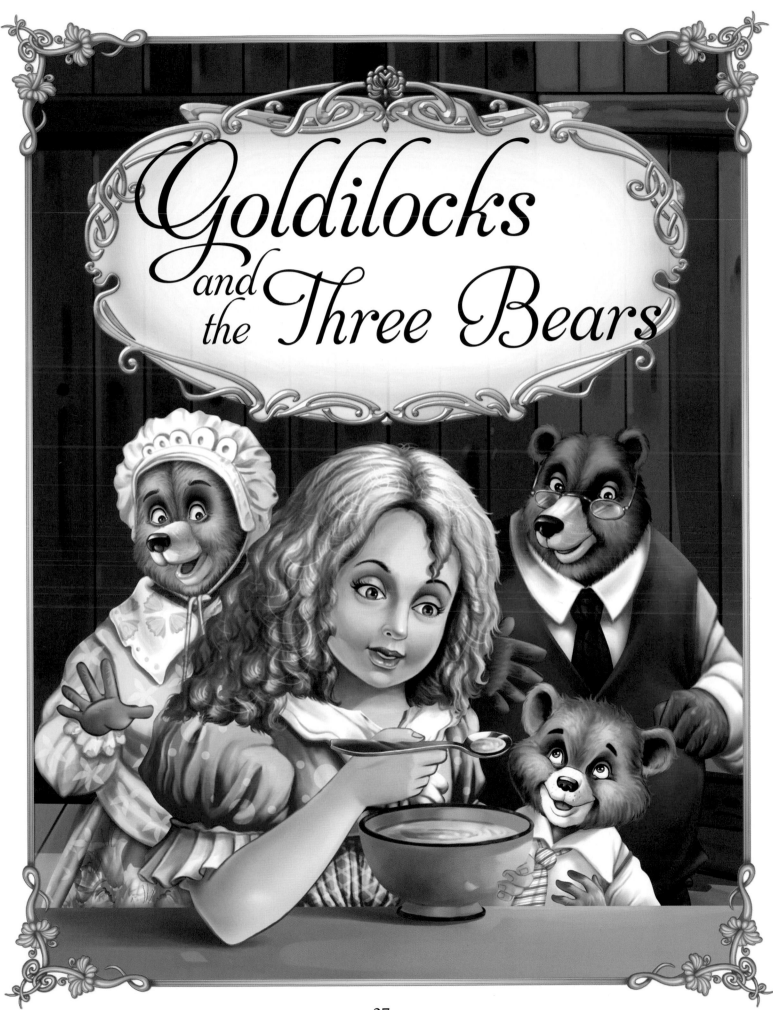

Goldilocks
and the Three Bears

Once upon a time there were three bears who lived together in a house in the woods. One of them was a Father Bear, one was a Mother Bear and the other was a Baby Bear.

They each had a bowl for their porridge: a big bowl for Father Bear, a medium-sized bowl for Mother Bear and a little bowl for Baby Bear. They each had a chair to sit on: a big chair for Father Bear, a medium-sized chair for Mother Bear and a little chair for Baby Bear. And they each had a bed to sleep in: a big bed for Father Bear, a medium-sized bed for Mother Bear and a little bed for Baby Bear.

One day, they made their porridge for breakfast and poured it into the porridge bowls. They decided to go for a walk in the woods while their porridge was cooling so they wouldn't burn their mouths. After all, they were sensible, well-brought-up bears.

While the bears were out walking, a little girl called Goldilocks passed by. She lived on the other side of the woods and had been sent on an errand by her mother. She saw the house and looked in the window. Goldilocks knocked on the door and then bent down and peered in the keyhole. She could see that no one was at home, so she lifted the latch and walked in.

Goldilocks was very pleased when she saw the bowls of porridge sitting on the table. Of course, most people would wait for the bears to come home and hope to be invited to breakfast. However, Goldilocks was rather spoiled and badly brought up, so she set about helping herself.

First she tried Father Bear's porridge, but that was too hot. Next she tried Mother Bear's porridge, but that was too cold. Then she tried Baby Bear's porridge, and that was neither too hot nor too cold. It was just right. Goldilocks liked it so much that she ate it all up.

Then Goldilocks felt tired, so she was pleased when she saw the three chairs. First she tried Father Bear's chair, but that was too hard. Next she tried Mother Bear's chair, but that was too soft. Then she tried Baby Bear's chair, and that was neither too hard nor too soft. It was just right. Goldilocks liked it so much that she sat in it until the chair gave way and she crashed down to the ground. That made her very cross.

Goldilocks was still feeling very tired, so she went upstairs to the bedroom, where she found the three beds. First she tried Father Bear's bed, but that was too hard. Next she tried Mother Bear's bed, but that was too soft. Then she tried Baby Bear's bed, and that was neither too hard nor too soft. It was just right. Goldilocks liked it so much that she pulled the covers over herself and fell fast asleep.

By this time, the three bears thought their porridge would be cool enough and came home to breakfast. When they went to the table, they saw that someone had left the spoons sitting in the porridge.

'Someone has been eating my porridge!' shouted Father Bear.

'Someone has been eating my porridge!' exclaimed Mother Bear.

'Someone has been eating my porridge, and they've eaten it all up!' cried Baby Bear.

The bears realised that somebody had been in their house, so they looked around to see if anything else had been disturbed. When they looked at the chairs, they saw that someone had moved the cushions on the seats around.

'Someone has been sitting in my chair!' shouted Father Bear.

'Someone has been sitting in my chair!' exclaimed Mother Bear.

'Someone has been sitting in my chair, and it's all broken!' cried Baby Bear.

The bears searched further, in case it was a burglar who had been in their house. They went upstairs to their bedroom and saw that the bedclothes on the beds were in disarray.

'Someone has been sleeping in my bed!' shouted Father Bear.

'Someone has been sleeping in my bed!' exclaimed Mother Bear.

'Someone has been sleeping in my bed, and they're still there!' cried Baby Bear.

Goldilocks got a terrible fright when she woke up and saw the three bears standing by the bed, looking at her. She jumped out of the other side of the bed and ran to the open window. She jumped out of the window and landed on the soft, springy grass below. She ran home as fast as she could.

The three bears never saw Goldilocks again, but she learnt her lesson about respecting the belongings of others. And the bears cooked a fresh batch of porridge and had their tasty breakfast!

HICKORY, DICKORY, DOCK

Hickory, dickory, dock,
The mouse ran up the clock,
The clock struck one,
The mouse ran down,
Hickory, dickory, dock.

THIS LITTLE PIGGY

This little piggy went to market,
This little piggy stayed at home;
This little piggy had roast beef,
This little piggy had none;
And this little piggy cried,
'Wee-wee-wee,'
All the way home.

OLD MCDONALD HAD A FARM

Old McDonald had a farm,
E-I-E-I-O!
And on that farm he had a cow,
E-I-E-I-O!
With a moo-moo here, and a moo-moo there,
Here a moo, there a moo,
Everywhere a moo-moo!
Old McDonald had a farm,
E-I-E-I-O!

Old McDonald had a farm,
E-I-E-I-O!
And on that farm he had a pig,
E-I-E-I-O!
With an oink-oink here, and an oink-oink there,
Here an oink, there an oink,
Everywhere an oink-oink!
Old McDonald had a farm,
E-I-E-I-O!

Old McDonald had a farm,
E-I-E-I-O!
And on that farm he had a horse,
E-I-E-I-O!
With a neigh-neigh here, and a neigh-neigh there,
Here a neigh, there a neigh,
Everywhere a neigh-neigh!
Old McDonald had a farm,
E-I-E-I-O!

Old McDonald had a farm,
E-I-E-I-O!
And on that farm he had some sheep,
E-I-E-I-O!
With a baa-baa here, and a baa-baa there,
Here a baa, there a baa,
Everywhere a baa-baa!
Old McDonald had a farm,
E-I-E-I-O!

Old McDonald had a farm,
E-I-E-I-O!
And on that farm he had a duck,
E-I-E-I-O!
With a quack-quack here,
and a quack-quack there,
Here a quack, there a quack,
Everywhere a quack-quack!
Old McDonald had a farm,
E-I-E-I-O!

Old McDonald had a farm,
E-I-E-I-O!
And on that farm he had a dog,
E-I-E-I-O!
With a woof-woof here,
and a woof-woof there,
Here a woof, there a woof,
Everywhere a woof-woof!
Old McDonald had a farm,
E-I-E-I-O!

HEY, DIDDLE, DIDDLE

Hey, diddle, diddle, the cat and the fiddle,
The cow jumped over the moon;
The little dog laughed to see such sport,
And the dish ran away with the spoon.

MONKEYS ON THE BED

Three little monkeys
   Jumping on the bed;
One fell off
And knocked his head.
Momma called the doctor,
The doctor said:
'No more monkeys
Jumping on the bed.'

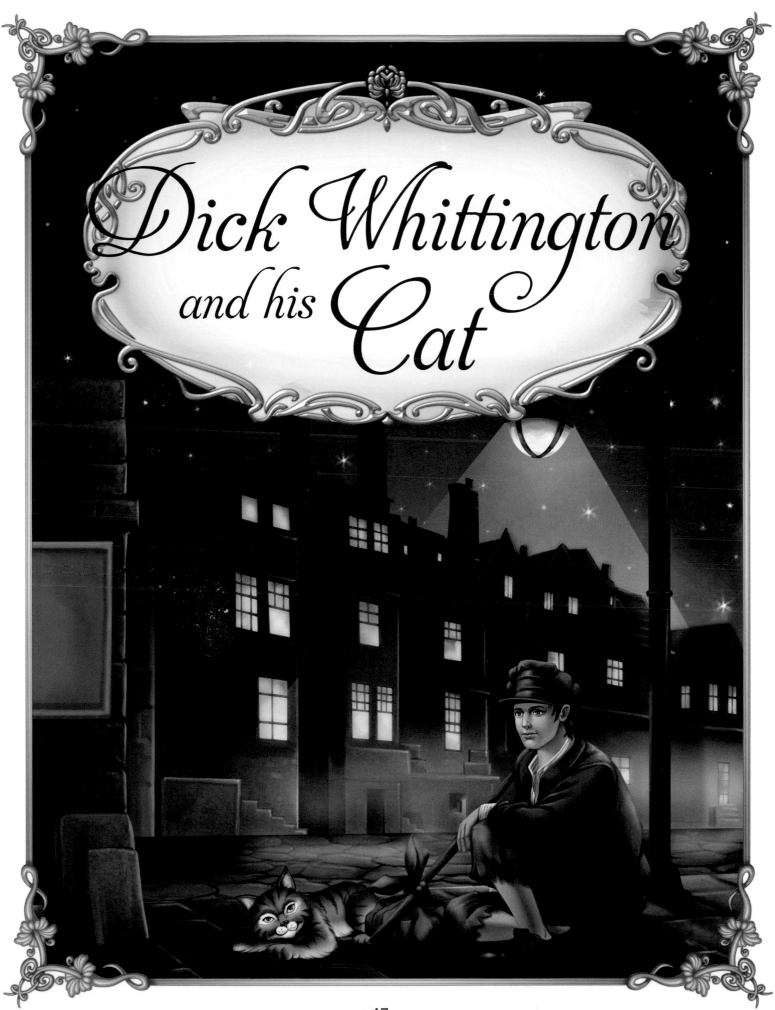

Dick Whittington and his Cat

Many years ago, there lived a boy named Dick Whittington. His parents died when he was very young, so he was very badly off. In those days country folk thought that the people of London were fine ladies and gentlemen who were so rich that the streets were paved with gold. Dick sat and listened to all these strange tales and longed to go to London and have fine clothes and lots to eat.

One day, a wagon with eight horses stopped in the village. Dick begged the driver to take him to London. The man felt sorry for Dick when he saw how ragged and poor he was. He agreed to take Dick, and they set off immediately.

Soon Dick found himself in the wonderful city he had heard so much about. But how disappointed he was! How dirty it seemed! He wandered up and down the streets, but not one was paved with gold. Instead, there was dirt everywhere.

Dick walked until it was dark. He sat down in a corner and fell asleep. When morning came, he was very cold and hungry, and although he asked everyone he met for help, only one or two gave him a halfpenny to buy some bread. For days, he lived on the streets, trying to find some work.

One day, he lay down in the doorway of a rich merchant named Fitzwarren. He was spotted by the cook, who was an unkind, bad-tempered woman. She cried out, 'Be off, lazy rogue, or I'll throw boiling hot, dirty dishwater over you!'

At that moment, Mr Fitzwarren came home for dinner. When he saw what was happening, he asked Dick why he had been lying there. 'You're old enough to work, my boy,' he said. 'I'm afraid you're just lazy.'

'But sir, that is not so,' Dick said. He told Mr Fitzwarren about his attempts to find work and described how hungry he was. Poor Dick was so weak that when he tried to stand, he fell down again. When the kind merchant saw this, he ordered that Dick be taken inside and given a good dinner. He said that Dick could stay and work in the kitchen, helping the cook.

Dick would have been happy if it weren't for the bad-tempered cook. She did her best to make life hard for Dick. She scolded him. Nothing he did was good enough. She even beat him with the broomstick or the ladle, or whatever else she had handy.

At last Miss Alice, Mr Fitzwarren's daughter, heard how badly the cook was treating Dick. She told the cook that she would lose her job if she didn't treat him more kindly, for the family had become quite fond of Dick.

After that the cook treated Dick better, but he had another problem. He slept in an attic that was overrun with rats and mice every night. Sometimes he hardly slept a wink. Luckily, one day he earned a penny for cleaning a gentleman's shoes. He then met a girl holding a cat and bought it with the penny. Puss soon saw that he had no more trouble with rats and mice, and he slept soundly every night.

One day, Mr Fitzwarren had a ship ready to sail. It was his custom to give his servants a chance to make their fortune, so he asked them what they wanted to send out on the ship to sell. They all had something to send except Dick, who had nothing. Miss Alice said, 'I will provide something for him,' but her father told her that it must be something of his own.

'I have nothing but my cat, which I bought for a penny,' Dick said.

'Go and fetch your cat then,' said Mr Fitzwarren.

Dick fetched poor Puss. There were tears in his eyes when he gave her to the ship's captain. They laughed at his odd goods, but Miss Alice, who felt sorry for him, gave Dick some money to buy another cat.

Miss Alice's acts of kindness made the cook jealous and she treated Dick worse than ever. She made fun of him for sending his cat to sea. 'Maybe the cat will sell for enough money to buy a stick to beat you with!' she mocked.

At last Dick could bear it no longer and ran away. He walked for a while and then sat down to rest. While he was sitting, the bells of the Bow Church began to chime. As they rang, it seemed they were singing over and over:

'Turn again, Whittington, Lord Mayor of London.'

'Lord Mayor of London!' he thought. 'Why, I'd put up with almost anything for that. I'll go back and ignore the nasty old cook.' And back he went.

Meanwhile, the ship travelled far away until it came to a foreign harbour where they had never seen a ship from England before. The King invited the captain to the palace for dinner, but no sooner were they seated than a horde of rats swarmed over the dishes and started devouring the food.

Thinking of the cat, the captain said he had a creature that would take care of the rats. The King was eager to see this wonderful animal. 'Bring it to me,' he said, 'for the vermin are unbearable. If it does what you say, I will load your ship with treasure.'

When the captain returned with Puss, the floor was still covered with rats. When she saw them, puss jumped down. In no time at all, most of the rats were dead and the rest ran off in fright. The King was delighted.

The King bought all the ship's cargo and gave the captain ten times as much for the cat as all the rest together.

Mr Fitzwarren was at his counting house when he heard a knock. It was the ship's captain with a chest of jewels. The captain told him about the cat and showed him the riches. Mr Fitzwarren told his servants to bring Dick but the servants hesitated, saying so great a treasure was too much for Dick. Good Mr Fitzwarren cried, 'Nonsense! The treasure belongs to him!'

He sent for Dick, who was black with dirt from scouring pots. At first, Dick thought they must be making fun of him. He begged them not to play tricks on a poor boy.

'We are not joking,' said the merchant. 'The captain has sold your cat and brings you more riches than I possess. Long may you enjoy them!'

Dick begged his master and Miss Alice to accept a share, but they refused. Dick was far too kind-hearted to keep it all to himself, so he gave some to the captain, the mate and the rest of Mr Fitzwarren's servants, and even to his old enemy, the cook.

Mr Fitzwarren advised him to send for some gentleman's clothes, and told him he was welcome to live in his house until he could find his own. When Dick's face was washed and he was dressed in a smart suit, he was as handsome and fine as any man who visited fair Alice Fitzwarren. She soon fell in love with him, and he with her.

A day for the wedding was arranged. They were married and afterwards treated everyone to a magnificent feast. History tells us that Mr Whittington and his lady lived in great splendour and were very happy. He became Sheriff, was made Lord Mayor of London four times, and received the honour of knighthood from the King.

POP GOES THE WEASEL!

Up and down the City Road,
In and out the Eagle,
That's the way the money goes,
Pop goes the weasel!

Half a pound of tuppenny rice,
Half a pound of treacle,
Mix it up and make it nice,
Pop goes the weasel!

Every night when I go out
The monkey's on the table,
Take a stick and knock it off,
Pop goes the weasel!

OH WHERE, OH WHERE, HAS MY LITTLE DOG GONE?

Oh where, oh where,
Has my little dog gone?
Oh where, oh where can he be?

With his ears cut short
And his tail cut long,
Oh where, oh where is he?

Puss in Boots

Once upon a time, there was an old miller who died, leaving nothing for his three sons apart from his mill, his donkey and his cat.

The three sons decided to split this poor property between themselves. The eldest son took the mill, the second son took the donkey and the youngest son received nothing but the cat.

Understandably, the youngest son was quite disappointed that his share was so poor. 'My brothers may make a handsome enough living if they combine their shares together,' said the youngest son, 'but, for my part, once I have eaten this cat and made a hat of his skin, I must die of hunger.'

The cat heard the youngest son saying all this, but he appeared to take no notice of it. Instead, he turned to his master with a grave and serious air and said, 'Do not worry yourself so, my master. All you have to do is give me a bag and get a pair of boots made for me so I may scamper easily through the thorns and brambles, and you shall soon see that, as my owner, you don't have such a poor share after all.'

Although the youngest son did not entirely trust what the cat had said, he remembered that he'd seen the cat play cunning tricks to catch rats and mice. The cat had hung himself by the heels to make the mice think he was dead and had hidden himself in the corn, so the cat's master did not completely despair of the cat helping him out of his situation.

Once his young master had given him his new boots and bag, the cat was very pleased. He thought he looked very gallant and elegant in his shiny boots. Wearing his new boots, the cat hung his bag around his neck and held its strings in his two forepaws. He went out into the fields and found some tender, juicy grass to put in the bag.

Then the cat went to a nearby rabbit warren where he knew a great number of rabbits lived. He stretched himself out on the ground as though he were dead, making sure that some of the grass in the bag was poking out. The cat lay there, waiting for some young rabbits, not yet acquainted with the tricks of the world, to come along and be tempted by the food in his bag.

The cat had barely lain himself down when a young and foolish rabbit hopped up. It sniffed at him, and then climbed into the bag to eat the tender grass. At once, the cat drew closed the strings, catching the rabbit unawares.

Proud of his catch, the cat headed off to the palace and asked to see the king. He was shown to the king's court, where he made a low bow to those assembled there.

'I have brought you, Sire, a rabbit from the warren of my noble lord and master, the Marquis of Carabas (which was the title that the cat was pleased to invent for his master),' said the cat. 'He commanded me to bring this to Your Majesty as a gift.'

The king was very pleased with the gift, as he was extremely fond of tasty rabbit.

'Tell thy master,' said the king, 'that I thank him and that I am well pleased with his gift.'

The cat departed, happy with the outcome of his endeavour.

Shortly after this, the cat hid himself amongst some tall corn in a field, again with his bag around his neck. He stood as still as a statue near the tastiest looking corn he could find and held his bag open. It wasn't long before two partridges came along and, in their efforts to eat the corn, fell into the open bag. At once, the cat drew the strings closed, catching both birds.

As he had done with the rabbit, the cat went to the palace and made a present of the partridges to the king. In the same way, the king received the partridges with great pleasure. The king even commanded his servants to reward the cat with a gold coin.

Over the course of the next two or three months, the cat continued to take some of his master's game as a gift to the king. The king was always very pleased to receive these offerings and he rewarded the cat with a gold coin.

One day, the cat discovered that the king was to go for a drive along the riverside to get some fresh air and enjoy the sunshine. The cat also discovered that the king was taking his daughter, the most beautiful princess in the world, with him on the drive.

The cat went to his master and said, 'If you will follow my advice, your fortune is made. You don't have to do anything apart from going to the river and having a bath at the spot that I show you. Just leave all the rest to me.'

The cat's master was confused as to why the cat was asking him to do this, but he did as the cat advised. While he was bathing, the king's carriage passed by.

At once, the cat cried out at the top of his voice, 'Help! Help! My master, the Marquis of Carabas, is drowning! Help! Help!'

Hearing the noise, the king looked out of the carriage window. Seeing the cat who had brought him so many gifts of game, he commanded his guards to immediately run to the assistance of his Lordship, the Marquis of Carabas.

As the king's guards were pulling the marquis out of the river, the cat hid his master's clothes under a large, heavy rock. Then the cat went up the coach and told the king that while his master was bathing, some thieves had come and stolen his clothes, even though the cat had cried out, 'Thieves! Thieves!' as loudly as he could. At once, the king commanded some guards to run and fetch one of his best suits for the Marquis of Carabas to wear.

70

The king was exceedingly polite to the marquis once he had put on the fine suit, as the clothes set off his good looks (for he was very handsome) and the king saw that his lovely daughter was very taken with the marquis. The marquis had only to exchange two or three respectful and tender glances with her before they found themselves in love. The king invited the marquis to join them on their drive.

The cat was overjoyed to see his plan succeeding. He marched on ahead of the coach and met some people mowing in a meadow, which was owned by a cruel ogre.

'Good mowers,' said the cat, 'the ogre who owns this field has asked me to tell you that if you do not tell the king that the meadow you are mowing belongs to the Marquis of Carabas, he will chop you up into tiny pieces and cook you in his pot!'

The mowers were very frightened of the ogre, so when the king drove past and asked them who owned the meadow, they all immediately answered, 'The Marquis of Carabas does, Your Majesty.'

'You have a fine meadow there,' the king said to the marquis.

'Yes Sire,' replied the marquis, thinking quickly. 'It gives me a good harvest every year.'

The cat continued on ahead, until he met with some reapers, who were harvesting corn in another field owned by the ogre.

'Good reapers,' said the cat, 'the ogre who owns this field has asked me to tell you that if you do not tell the king that this corn belongs to the Marquis of Carabas, he will chop you up into tiny pieces and cook you in his pot!'

And when the king passed the field in his carriage and asked them who owned it, they all replied, 'The Marquis of Carabas owns this corn, Your Majesty.'

The cat went on ahead again and told everyone he met that the ogre said to tell the King that the land was owned by the Marquis of Carabas. Everyone was so scared of the ogre that they did.

Eventually the cat came to the ogre's home, which was an enormous, stately castle. The ogre was the richest ogre ever known. The cat, who had discovered the ogre's magical talent, asked to see him, saying he couldn't pass by without paying his respects. After some grumbling, the ogre let him in and made him sit down.

'I have been told that you have an amazing gift,' said the cat to the ogre. 'They tell me that you can change yourself into any creature you choose, such as a lion. Surely this is not true?'

'It is true! If you don't believe me, let me prove it to you,' said the proud ogre, and he turned himself into a fierce, snarling lion.

The cat seemed so terrified at the sight of the lion that he jumped up and tried to climb on to a cupboard, which was rather awkward because of his boots. When he saw the ogre had finally returned to his normal form, he slowly climbed down.

'That is impressive!' said the cat. 'But I have also been told that you can take on the shape of the smallest animal, such as a mouse. Surely, though, that is impossible.'

'Impossible?' roared the ogre. 'Watch and you shall see!'

And the ogre changed himself into a tiny mouse and began to run around the room. The cat immediately sprung on him and ate him up!

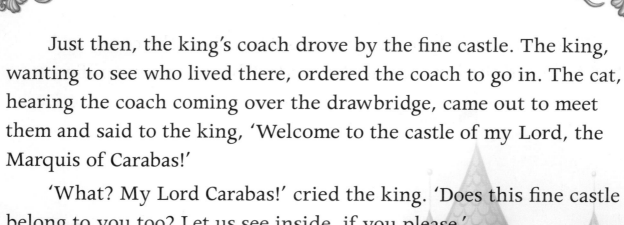

Just then, the king's coach drove by the fine castle. The king, wanting to see who lived there, ordered the coach to go in. The cat, hearing the coach coming over the drawbridge, came out to meet them and said to the king, 'Welcome to the castle of my Lord, the Marquis of Carabas!'

'What? My Lord Carabas!' cried the king. 'Does this fine castle belong to you too? Let us see inside, if you please.'

The marquis helped the princess down from the coach and they followed the king inside the castle. There was a magnificent feast prepared in the Great Hall for the ogre. The king was perfectly charmed with the fine qualities of the marquis, as was the princess, who had fallen completely in love with him.

The king could see that his daughter was in love with the marquis and he was so impressed on seeing the vast estates and fine castle that the marquis owned that he insisted that the marquis and the princess get married that very day.

They lived happily ever after, and the cat became a great lord. He never had to chase mice again, although he sometimes did for fun!

A WISE OLD OWL

A wise old owl lived in an oak,
The more he saw the less he spoke;
The less he spoke the more he heard.
Why aren't we all like that wise old bird?

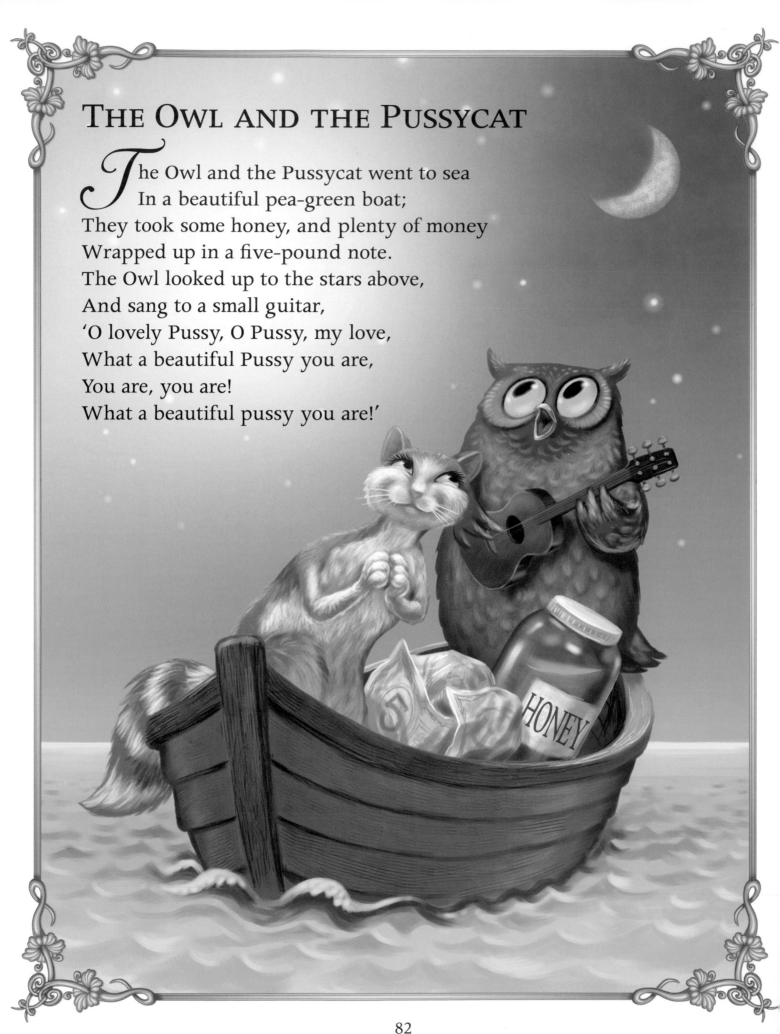

THE OWL AND THE PUSSYCAT

The Owl and the Pussycat went to sea
    In a beautiful pea-green boat;
They took some honey, and plenty of money
Wrapped up in a five-pound note.
The Owl looked up to the stars above,
And sang to a small guitar,
'O lovely Pussy, O Pussy, my love,
What a beautiful Pussy you are,
You are, you are!
What a beautiful pussy you are!'

Pussy said to the Owl, 'You elegant fowl,
How charmingly sweet you sing!
O, let us be married;
   too long have we tarried:
But what shall we do for a ring?'
They sailed away, for a year and a day,
To the land where the bong-tree grows,
And there in a wood a Piggy-wig stood,
With a ring at the end of his nose,
His nose, his nose,
With a ring at the end of his nose.

'Dear Pig, are you willing to sell for one shilling
Your ring?' Said the Piggy, 'I will.'
So they took it away, and were married next day
By the turkey who lives on the hill.
They dined on mince and slices of quince,
Which they ate with a runcible spoon;
And hand in hand, on the edge of the sand,
They danced by the light of the moon,
The moon, the moon,
They danced by the light of the moon.

Edward Lear

HICKETY, PICKETY

Hickety, pickety, my black hen,
She lays eggs for gentlemen;
Gentlemen come every day
To see what my black hen doth lay;
Sometimes nine and sometimes ten,
Hickety, pickety, my black hen.

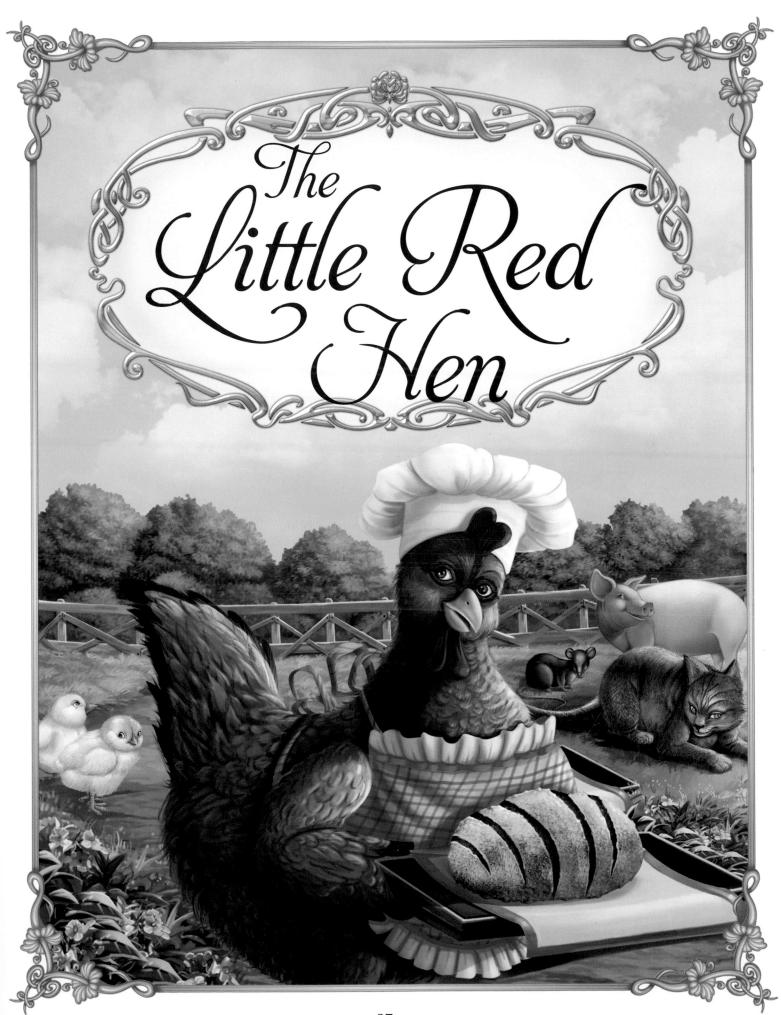

The Little Red Hen

The Little Red Hen lived in the barnyard with her chicks. She spent her time walking about in her picketty-pecketty way, scratching the ground and looking for worms to feed her family. She loved juicy, fat worms and whenever she found one, she would call out 'Chuck-chuck-chuck!' to her chicks, who would come running. She would share out her find and then it was back to her picketty-pecketty scratching, looking for more.

A Cat usually napped lazily away next to the barn door in the sun, not even bothering to chase the Rat, who ran here and there as he pleased. As for the Pig who lived in the sty, he did not care about anything, as long as he could eat and get fat.

One summer day as she was scratching away, the Little Red Hen found a seed sitting in the dust. She discovered it was a wheat seed. If it was planted, it would grow seeds that could be made into flour and turned into bread.

The Little Red Hen thought of the Cat, who slept all day, and the Rat, who did as he pleased, and the Pig, whose only concern was his food. She called out loudly to them, 'Who will plant this seed?'

But the Cat meowed, 'Not I,' and the Rat squeaked, 'Not I,' and the Pig grunted, 'Not I.'

'Well then,' said the Little Red Hen, 'I will.'

And she did.

Then she went about her duties, scratching for worms in her picketty-pecketty way and feeding her chicks, while the Cat grew fat, and the Rat grew fat, and the Pig grew fat. Meanwhile, the wheat grew tall.

One day, the Little Red Hen decided that the wheat was grown and ripe, ready for harvest. She called out loudly, 'Who will harvest the wheat?'

But the Cat meowed, 'Not I,' and the Rat squeaked, 'Not I,' and the Pig grunted, 'Not I.'

'Well then,' said the Little Red Hen, 'I will.'

And she did.

She went and got the farmer's sickle from his tools in the barn and harvested the wheat in her picketty-pecketty way. The nicely cut wheat lay on the ground, but her little yellow chicks crowded around her, 'peep-peep-peeping' for attention, crying that their mother was neglecting them.

Poor Little Red Hen! She didn't know what to do. She was divided between her duty to her chicks and her duty to the wheat. So, hoping for some help, she called out, 'Who will thresh the wheat?'

But the Cat meowed, 'Not I,' and the Rat squeaked, 'Not I,' and the Pig grunted, 'Not I.'

'Well then,' said the Little Red Hen, 'I will.'

And she did.

Of course, she first went a-hunting worms for her children and made sure that they were all fed and happy. When they were all asleep for their afternoon nap, she went out and threshed the wheat.

Then she called out, 'Who will carry the wheat to the mill to be ground into flour?'

But the Cat meowed, 'Not I,' and the Rat squeaked, 'Not I,' and the Pig grunted, 'Not I.'

'Well then,' said the Little Red Hen, 'I will.'

And she did.

The Little Red Hen loaded up the wheat in a sack and headed off to the mill, far away. The miller ground her wheat into beautiful flour and she trudged back again in her picketty-pecketty way. She even managed, in spite of the load, to catch a juicy worm or two for her chicks. She was so tired when she returned that she went to sleep early.

The Little Red Hen would have loved to sleep late but her chicks woke her, 'peep-peep-peeping' for their breakfast. As she woke, she remembered that today was the day to make the flour into bread. After her children were fed, she went looking for the Cat, the Rat and the Pig. She called out, 'Who will make the bread?'

But the Cat meowed, 'Not I,' and the Rat squeaked, 'Not I,' and the Pig grunted, 'Not I.'

'Well then,' said the Little Red Hen, 'I will.'

And she did.

She put on a fresh apron and a white cook's hat and followed the recipe. She made the dough and kneaded it and shaped it into loaves and put them in the oven to bake.

At last, the bread was ready. A delicious smell wafted across the barnyard. The Cat, the Rat and the Pig all sniffed the air with delight. The Little Red Hen went over to the oven in her picketty-pecketty way. She was very excited about the wonderful bread, which is not surprising, for had she not done all the work?

The Little Red Hen opened the oven and found that the lovely brown loaves of bread were cooked to perfection. Then, out of habit, she called out, 'Who will eat the bread?'

And the Cat meowed, 'I will,' and the Rat squeaked, 'I will,' and the Pig grunted, 'I will.'

But the Little Red Hen said, 'No, you won't. I will.'

And she did!

I HAD A LITTLE HEN

I had a little hen,
   The prettiest ever seen;
She washed up the dishes,
And kept the house clean.
She went to the mill
To fetch me some flour,
She brought it home
In less than an hour.
She baked me my bread,
She brewed me my ale,
She sat by the fire
And told many a fine tale.

LITTLE BO-PEEP

Little Bo-Peep has lost her sheep,
And can't tell where to find them;
Leave them alone, and they'll come home,
And bring their tails behind them.

Little Bo-Peep fell fast asleep,
And dreamed she heard them bleating;
But when she awoke she found it a joke,
For they were still a-fleeting.

Then up she took her little crook,
Determined for to find them;
She found them indeed, but it made her heart bleed,
For they'd left their tails behind them.

It happened one day, as Bo-Peep did stray
Into a meadow hard by,
There she spied their tails side by side,
All hung on a tree to dry.

She heaved a sigh, and wiped her eye,
And over the hillocks went rambling,
And tried what she could, as a shepherdess should,
To tack each again to its lambkin.

GOOSEY, GOOSEY GANDER

Goosey, goosey gander,
  Whither shall I wander?
Upstairs and downstairs
And in my lady's chamber;
There I met an old man
Who would not say his prayers;
I took him by the left leg
And threw him down the stairs.

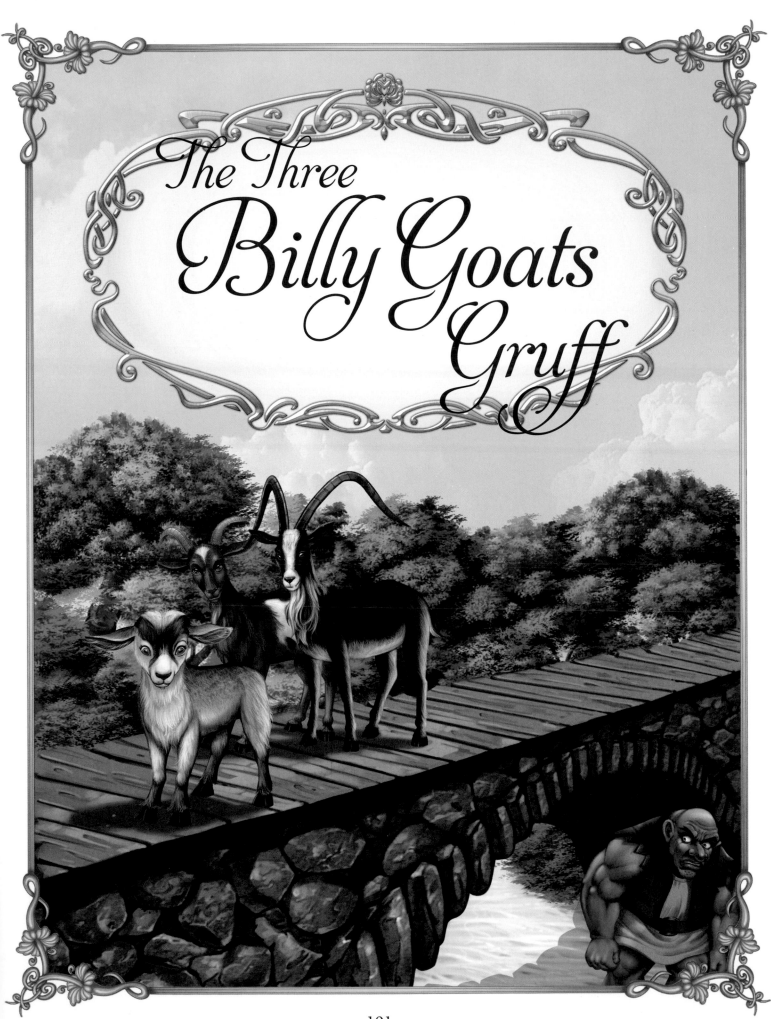

The Three Billy Goats Gruff

Once upon a time there lived on a hillside three billy goats whose name was Gruff.

Winter had passed and the lean, hungry billy goats wanted to go to the green meadow on the other side of the valley so they could eat the juicy, tasty grass and grow fat over the summer. At the bottom of the valley was a cascading stream that they had to cross. Over the stream was a bridge, but under the bridge there lived a great, ugly Troll, with eyes like big, round saucers and a nose as long as a poker.

First of all went the youngest and smallest Billy Goat Gruff.

'Trip, trip, trip, trip!' went the wooden bridge as the billy goat's hoofs danced across it.

'Who's that tripping over my bridge?' roared the Troll from underneath the bridge.

'It's me, the tiniest Billy Goat Gruff,' said the billy goat in a tiny voice. 'I am going up the hillside to eat some juicy, tasty grass so I can grow fat!'

'No you're not!' roared the Troll. 'I am coming to gobble you up!'

'Oh, please don't eat me! I'm too little, I am,' said the youngest Billy Goat Gruff. 'If you wait a little while longer, the second Billy Goat Gruff will come along. He's much bigger than me.'

'Bigger, is he?' asked the hungry Troll. 'Well, be off with you then!'

And the youngest Billy Goat Gruff tripped lightly across the bridge to the meadow.

After a little while, the second Billy Goat Gruff came along to cross the bridge. He was a medium-sized billy goat.

'Trap, trap, trap, trap!' went the wooden bridge as the second billy goat made his way across.

'Who's that trapping over my bridge?' roared the Troll from underneath the bridge.

'It's me, the second Billy Goat Gruff,' said the billy goat in a medium-sized voice. 'I am going up the hillside to eat some juicy, tasty grass so I can grow fat!'

'No you're not!' roared the Troll. 'I am coming to gobble you up!'

'Oh, please don't eat me! I'm only medium-sized, I am,' said the second Billy Goat Gruff. 'If you wait a little while longer, the third Billy Goat Gruff will come along. He's much bigger than me.'

'Bigger, is he?' asked the hungry Troll. 'Well, be off with you then!'

And the second Billy Goat Gruff trapped across the bridge to the meadow.

Then the third Billy Goat Gruff came along to cross the bridge. He was a very large billy goat.

'Tramp, tramp, tramp, tramp!' went the wooden bridge as the third billy goat stomped across it.

'Who's that tramping over my bridge?' roared the Troll from underneath the bridge.

'It's me, the third Billy Goat Gruff!' roared the billy goat in a very loud voice. I am going up the hillside to eat some juicy, tasty grass so I can grow fat!'

'No you're not!' roared the Troll, jumping up on to the bridge. 'I am coming to gobble you up!'

'Well, come along then!' said the third Billy Goat Gruff. He lowered his head and pointed his horns at the Troll. Then he charged!

The Troll bounced into the air and landed on the bridge. The big billy goat jumped on to the troll and stomped him with his big hoofs. Then he kicked out his hind legs and tossed the Troll into the rapids below. The Troll floated away, black and blue, and that was the last anyone ever saw of him.

The three Billy Goats Gruff went up the hillside to the green meadow. There they ate some juicy, tasty grass until they were so fat that they could scarcely walk home again. And after that day, they went to the meadow on the opposite side of the valley whenever they wished.

HIGGLETY, PIGGLETY, POP!

Higglety, pigglety, pop!
  The dog has eaten the mop;
The pig's in a hurry,
The cat's in a flurry,
Higglety, pigglety, pop!

OLD MOTHER HUBBARD

Old Mother Hubbard
　　Went to the cupboard
To fetch her poor dog a bone;
But when she got there,
The cupboard was bare,
And so the poor dog had none.

She went to the baker's
To buy him some bread;
But when she came back
The poor dog was dead.

She went to the undertaker's
To buy him a coffin;
But when she came back
The poor dog was laughing.

She went to the fishmonger's
To buy him some fish;
But when she came back
He was washing the dish.

She went to the tavern
For white wine and red;
But when she came back
The dog stood on his head.

She went to the hatter's
To buy him a hat;
But when she came back
He was feeding the cat.

She went to the barber's
To buy him a wig;
But when she came back,
He was dancing a jig.

She went to the fruiterer's
To buy him some fruit;
But when she came back,
He was playing the flute.

She went to the tailor's
To buy him a coat;
But when she came back
He was riding a goat.

She went to the cobbler's
To buy him some shoes,
But when she came back
He was reading the news.

She went to the seamstress
To buy him some linen;
But when she came back
The dog was a-spinning.

She went to the hosier's
To buy him some hose;
But when she came back
He was dressed in his clothes.

The dame made a curtsy,
The dog made a bow;
The dame said, 'Your servant!'
The dog said, 'Bow-wow.'

BAA, BAA, BLACK SHEEP

Baa, baa, black sheep,
Have you any wool?
Yes, sir, yes, sir,
Three bags full;
One for the master,
And one for the dame,
And one for the little boy
Who lives down the lane.

The Musicians of Bremen

A farmer once owned an old donkey. The donkey had worked faithfully for his master for many years. He'd carried huge sacks of wheat up the hill to the mill and bags of flour back down again, pulled heavily laden carts great distances and been ridden into town and back by the farmer's wife and children.

As he grew older, the poor donkey's strength began to fail him and he was no longer able to perform all the tasks that the farmer set him. With each day that passed, the donkey became more and more unfit for the hard work for which the farmer needed him.

At last, the farmer decided that it was time for him to get rid of the poor old donkey, as he could not afford to keep the beast if he could not perform his duties. However, the old donkey overheard the farmer talking to his wife about whether he should turn the donkey out or put an end to him. The donkey, guessing that his future at the farm looked grim, decided he would run away.

After some thought, the donkey resolved that he would take the road to the town of Bremen, famous for its freedom, where he could make his own living as a town musician. So off he headed down the road to that great city.

After the donkey had walked for a little way, he came across a dog lying down next to the road. The dog was panting as though he was tired after running a long distance.

'Hello friend,' said the donkey. 'Why are you panting and so out of breath?'

'Alas!' replied the dog. 'Now that I'm old and getting weaker all the time, my master has decided that I can no longer make myself useful when he's hunting. He decided get rid of me, but I escaped and ran away. I've been travelling such a long way, but I have no idea how I am going to earn my livelihood.'

'I've got an idea,' said the donkey. 'My master was also going to get rid of me because I was getting too old to work for him. I have also run away and I am making my way to Bremen, where I will become a town musician. Why don't you join me and we shall earn our living by making music together?'

The dog happily agreed, and so the two animals continued down the road together, talking about their plans to become musicians.

After the donkey and the dog had gone a little further, they spied a cat sitting by the road, looking as miserable as a cat could possibly look.

'Hello dear lady,' said the donkey. 'Why do you look so very sad?'

'You'd look miserable too if you were in danger of being thrown in the well,' replied the cat. 'Now that I am getting old, my teeth and claws are becoming blunt. I'd much prefer to lie by the kitchen fire and purr and sleep instead of running about the house chasing mice all day. My mistress was going to get rid of me because I was of no further use to her, so I ran away. But now I don't know what is going to become of me.'

'Why don't you come with us to Bremen?' suggested the donkey. 'The dog and I have also run away from our masters because we are too old and so we are going to try earning our way by becoming town musicians. You are bound to be an excellent night-time singer!'

The cat was very pleased with this idea and so the three animals continued down the road together towards Bremen.

The donkey, dog and cat had walked a little further when they saw a rooster perched on a farm gate. He was loudly crowing with all his might, creating an enormous racket.

'Bravo!' cried the donkey. 'What a wonderful performance! But tell me, why are you making all this fuss?'

'I have been a good rooster and foretold fine weather for wash-day,' said the rooster, 'but instead of getting any thanks, I heard that my mistress has company coming for Sunday lunch. She has told the cook to cut off my head tomorrow and cook me in a soup for them to eat! So here I am, crowing with all my might while I still can.'

'Goodness me!' exclaimed the donkey. 'You had better come along with us, good sir. Anything would be better than staying to have your head removed! Who knows? If we can all sing in tune, your powerful voice will be a very pleasing addition to our performance.'

The rooster was very happy to accept this offer and so he joined them on their travels to Bremen. The four animals went on down the road together, quite jolly.

However, as they went along, the four friends realised that they could not reach Bremen in one day. As night approached, the travellers came to a wood. They talked together and decided that they would spend the night in the woods and then continue on to Bremen the next morning.

The donkey and the dog lay down to sleep on the ground under a great tree. The cat climbed up into the branches of the tree for her rest. The rooster flew up to the top of the tree, as that was the safest place for him to perch for the night.

As was his habit, the rooster looked around on all sides to make sure all was well before he settled down to sleep. As he was looking out into the wood, the rooster spied a little light off through the trees, bright and shining.

'I see a light!' the rooster called down to his friends. 'There must be a house nearby, as the light does not seem very far away!'

'If that is so,' said the donkey, 'it would be best if we got up and investigated. After all, this wood is not the best place to sleep, especially when there is somewhere close by that might be much better! They might have a nice warm stable and some fresh hay for me to munch on.'

'I wouldn't mind a bone or two either, or a bit of meat to eat,' said the dog.

'Maybe there's a cosy basket by the fire and a piece of fish to dine on,' said the cat.

'Or a snug hen house with some tasty corn for me to peck at,' said the rooster.

So the four friends decided they would seek out better quarters for the night. They set off together into the woods towards where the rooster had seen the light.

As they came closer, the light shone brighter and brighter until they could see a snug little house, all lit up. Now, it turned out that this was a house in which a gang of fearsome robbers lived.

The donkey, being the tallest, went up to the window and peeked in. 'Well, donkey, what do you see?' asked the dog.

'What do I see? I see a large table laid out with all kinds of splendid things to eat,' replied the donkey. 'I also see a gang of robbers sitting around the table, eating and drinking and looking very comfortable.'

'That sounds like it would be very suitable for us,' said the rooster.

'Yes indeed,' said the donkey. 'Now if only we could get in there.'

The four friends consulted together on the best way to get the robbers out of the house. After a great deal of discussion, they hit on a plan.

The donkey stood up on his hind legs with his front legs resting on the window sill for support. The dog climbed up on to the donkey's back and then the cat scrambled up on to the dog's shoulders. Finally, the rooster flew up and perched himself on top of the cat's head.

When they were all ready, the donkey gave a signal and the animals began to perform their music. The donkey brayed loudly, the dog barked furiously, the cat meowed at the top of her voice and the rooster crowed deafeningly.

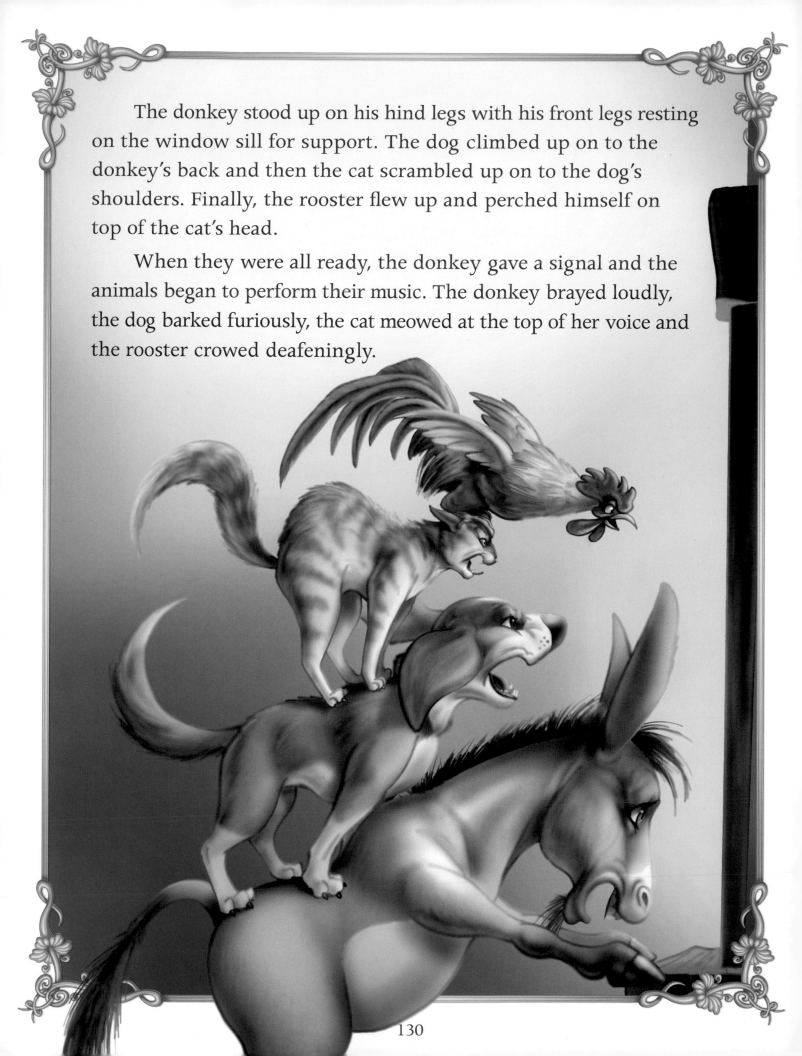

Then, the four animals crashed in through the window, tumbling amongst the broken glass with a hideous clatter! The robbers, who had already been alarmed by the noisy performance, thought some terrible goblin must be after them, and they all took to their heels and fled into the woods.

Once the coast was clear, the four friends sat down at the table and finished the robbers' splendid meal, feasting as if they hadn't seen food for a month.

When they had finished their meal, they put out the lights and each found a place to sleep. The donkey lay down outside in the yard on a pile of straw; the dog stretched out on a mat behind the front door; the cat curled up on the hearth in front of the ashes of the fire; and the rooster settled himself down on a beam in the ceiling. They soon fell asleep, as they were very tired from their long journey.

As midnight drew near, the robbers, who were watching from afar, saw that no light was burning in their cottage. As it all seemed quiet and still, they thought that maybe they had been in too much of a hurry to run away. The captain, worried that they'd left their lair for no reason, instructed one of the thieves to go back to the cottage and investigate.

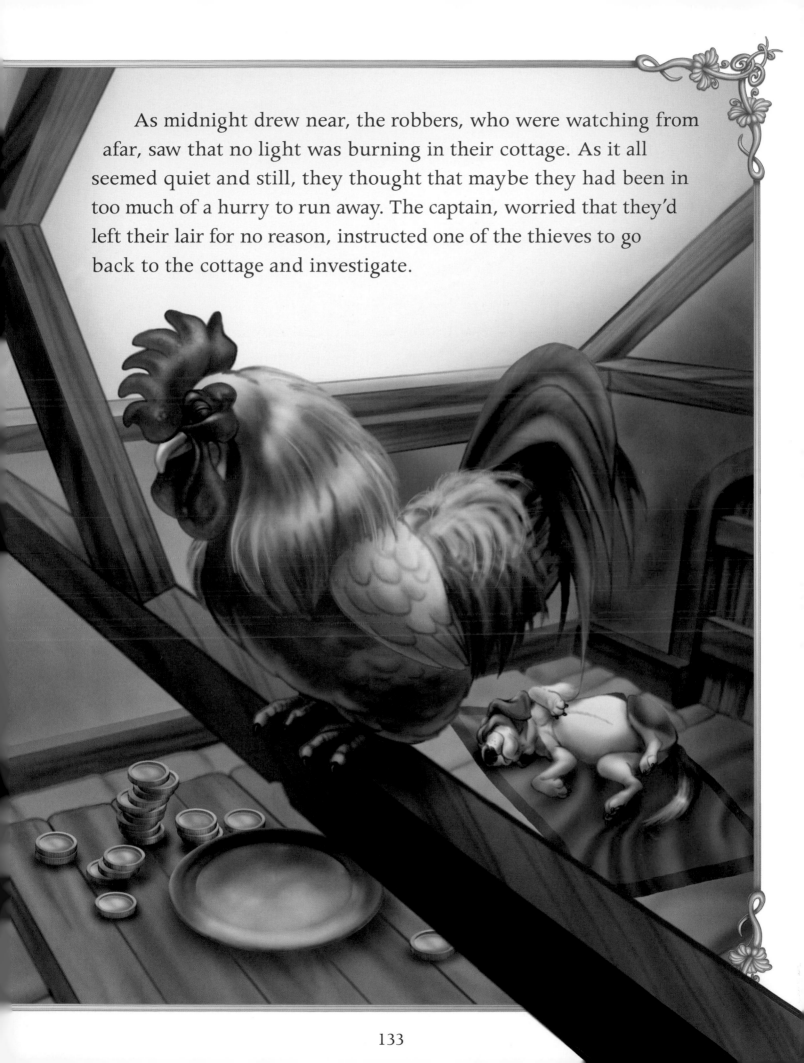

The robber crept up to the cottage and peered in the windows. Seeing nothing inside and finding that everything was quiet, he made his way into the dark kitchen. The robber groped around in the dark, trying to find a match so he could light a candle. Hearing a noise, the cat, who had been sleeping in front of the fireplace, woke up and opened her eyes.

The robber spied the glittering eyes of the cat, but he mistook them for burning coals in the fireplace. He stumbled forward, holding out the match to try and light it with the coals, but he only succeeded in poking the poor cat in the face. At once, the cat flew into a rage and jumped up, spitting and scratching the unfortunate robber in the face with her claws.

The frightened robber cried out in terror and ran to the front door, but he stumbled over the dog, who was woken by all the noise. At once, the dog jumped up, growling furiously and biting the robber's ankles and legs with his sharp teeth.

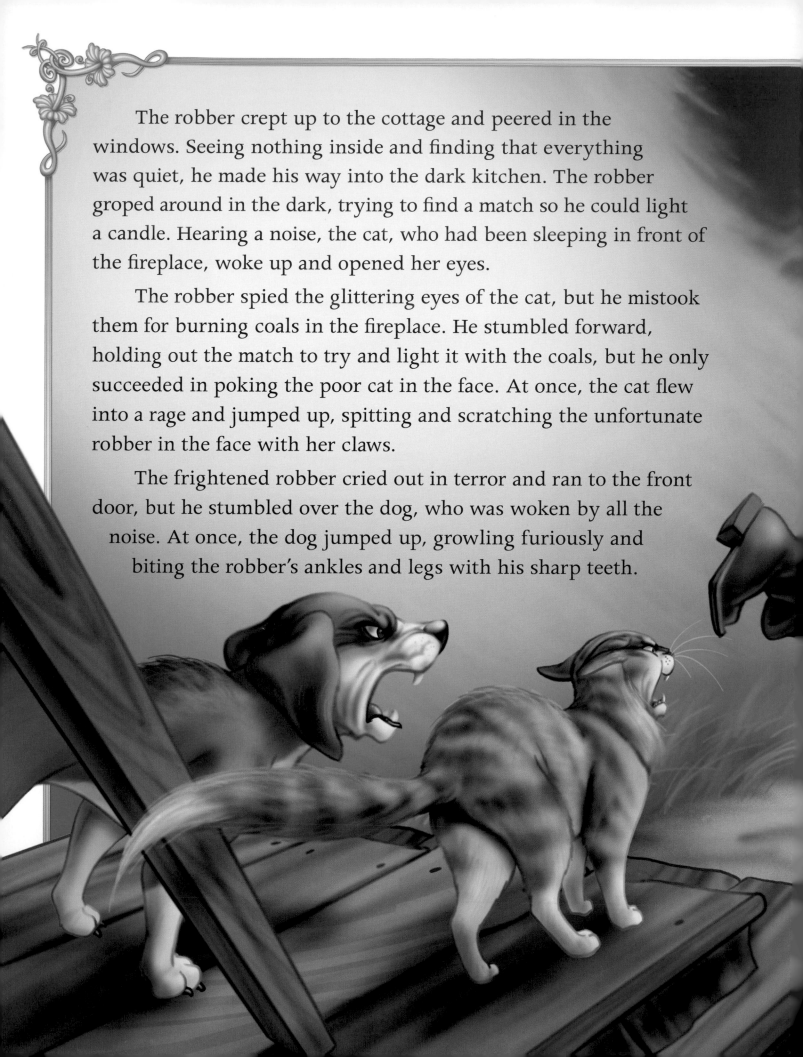

The ill-fated robber ran out the door into the yard, bumping into the donkey, who had got up to investigate what all the fuss was about. The donkey kicked out at the robber with his hind legs, catching the fellow squarely in his chest.

All this time, the rooster, who had also been awoken by the noise, stood in the rafters, crowing out 'Cock-a-doodle-doo!' at the top of his voice.

The robber ran back to his gang as fast as he could to make his report to the captain.

'It was awful!' the robber cried. 'I went into the kitchen, where I was attacked by a horrid witch who spat and scratched at me with her long sharp fingernails!"

The robber paused for breath before continuing.

'As I ran out of the house, I was attacked by a man standing behind the door who stabbed me in my leg with a sharp knife!' he said.

He paused to show his colleagues his bleeding leg.

'Then I fled out into the yard,' said the robber, 'where I ran into a huge black monster, who rose up in front of me and struck me with his huge, heavy club!'

The other gang members gasped as they looked at the robber's bruises.

'Finally, as I ran away, a devil cried out from the roof of the house. "Throw that rascal up to me!" it shrieked. I ran away as fast as I could and I'm never going back there!' the frightened robber finished.

From that time on, the robbers never dared to go back to the house. The four travellers were so pleased with their new quarters that they set up house there and never made it to Bremen. And there they are, it is said, until this very day.

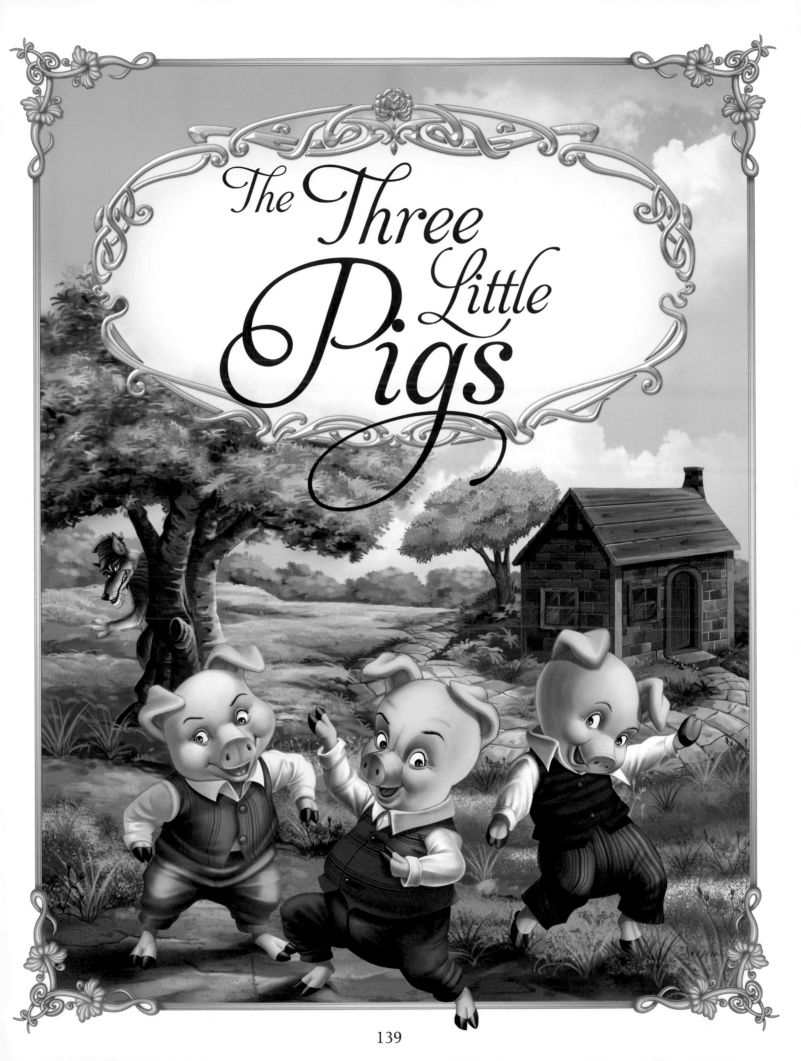

The Three Little Pigs

Once upon a time there lived a mother sow with her Three Little Pigs. As she did not have enough money to look after them she sent them out into the world to seek their fortunes.

As he was walking down the road, the First Little Pig met a man carrying a bundle of straw. 'Please, sir, give me that straw so I can build a house with it.'

The man gave the straw to the First Little Pig, who went and built a house with it.

As he was walking down the road, the Second Little Pig met a man carrying a bundle of sticks. 'Please, sir, give me those sticks so I can build a house with them.'

The man gave the sticks to the Second Little Pig, who went and built a house with them.

As he was walking down the road, the Third Little Pig met a man carrying a pile of bricks. 'Please, sir, give me those bricks so I can build a house with them.'

The man gave the bricks to the Third Little Pig, who went and built a house with them.

The Three Little Pigs lived happily until one day when a big bad Wolf came to the house of straw. The Wolf knocked at the door of the house made of straw and said, 'Little Pig, Little Pig, let me come in!'

The First Little Pig replied, 'No, not by the hair of my chinny chin chin!'

'Then I'll huff and I'll puff and I'll blow your house in!' cried the Wolf.

So the big bad Wolf huffed and he puffed and he blew down the house of straw. The First Little Pig ran as fast as he could to his brother's house of sticks.

Presently the big bad Wolf came to the house of sticks. The Wolf knocked at the door of the house made of sticks and said, 'Little Pig, Little Pig, let me come in!'

The First Little Pig and the Second Little Pig replied, 'No, not by the hair of my chinny chin chin!'

'Then I'll huff and I'll puff and I'll blow your house in!' cried the Wolf.

So the big bad Wolf huffed and he puffed and he huffed and he puffed and he blew down the house of sticks. The First Little Pig and the Second Little Pig ran as fast as they could to their brother's house of bricks.

Presently the big bad Wolf came to the house of bricks.
The Wolf knocked at the door of the house made of bricks
and said, 'Little Pig, Little Pig, let me come in!'

The First Little Pig and the Second Little Pig and the Third
Little Pig replied, 'No, not by the hair of my chinny chin chin!'

'Then I'll huff and I'll puff and I'll blow your house in!' cried
the Wolf.

So the big bad Wolf huffed and he puffed and he huffed and
he puffed and he huffed and he puffed but he could not blow down
the house of bricks.

When the Wolf realised that he could not blow down the house of bricks with his huffing and puffing, he said, 'Little Pig, I know where there is a nice field of juicy, tasty turnips.'

'Where?' asked the Third Little Pig.

'In Farmer Brown's field,' replied the Wolf. 'I will call for you at six o'clock tomorrow morning and we will go together to get some for our dinner.'

The next morning the clever Third Little Pig got up at five o'clock and went by himself to get the turnips. 'Are you ready to get some turnips?' asked the Wolf, when he arrived at the Pig's house at six o'clock.

'Ready? I have already been and come back with a nice potful for my dinner!' replied the Third Little Pig.

The Wolf was very angry. He said, 'Little Pig, I know where there is a nice apple tree.'

'Where?' asked the Third Little Pig.

'In Farmer Smith's orchard,' replied the Wolf. 'I will call for you at five o'clock tomorrow morning, and we will go together to get some juicy, tasty apples.'

However, the clever Third Little Pig got up at four o'clock and went to the apple tree. As he had further to go he was still up the tree picking apples when he saw the angry Wolf coming.

'Little Pig come down and tell me if they are nice apples,' called the wolf.

'They're very nice,' replied the Third Little Pig. 'Here, let me throw you one.' And he threw an apple so far that the Wolf had to go a long way to pick it up and the Little Pig was able to jump down and run home.

The next day the Wolf came and said to the Third Little Pig, 'Little Pig, there is a fair in town. Will you go with me at three o'clock this afternoon?'

'Very well,' said the Third Little Pig.

The Third Little Pig went off earlier to the fair and had a lovely time. He bought a butter churn and was heading home when he saw the Wolf coming. In a panic, he crawled inside the butter churn to hide and it fell over. Down the hill it rolled. When he saw the churn rolling towards him, the Wolf ran away in fright.

The Wolf went to the Third Little Pig's house and told him how he'd been frightened by a great round thing rolling down the hill towards him.

'Dear me, I hid inside the butter churn when I saw you coming and it rolled down the hill. I'm sorry I frightened you,' said the Third Little Pig.

The Wolf grew angry and swore that he would come down the chimney and eat up the First Little Pig and the Second Little Pig and the Third Little Pig. But while he was climbing on to the roof, the Third Little Pig made a blazing fire and put a big pot of water on to boil. As the Wolf was climbing down the chimney the Third Little Pig took off the lid and – splash! – the Wolf fell into the scalding water.

The Wolf howled and leapt so high that he jumped right out of the chimney. He ran off down the road as fast as he could. The Three Little Pigs lived happily ever after in the house of bricks and never saw the big bad Wolf again.

THREE BLIND MICE

Three blind mice, see how they run!
They all ran after the farmer's wife,
Who cut off their tails with a carving knife;
Did you ever see such a thing in your life,
As three blind mice?

FIVE LITTLE DUCKS

Five little ducks went out one day
  Over the hills and far away.
Mother duck said, 'Quack quack, quack quack!'
But only four little ducks came back.

Four little ducks went out one day
Over the hills and far away.
Mother duck said, 'Quack quack, quack quack!'
But only three little ducks came back.

Three little ducks went out one day
Over the hills and far away.
Mother duck said, 'Quack quack, quack quack!'
But only two little ducks came back.

Two little ducks went out one day
Over the hills and far away.
Mother duck said, 'Quack quack, quack quack!'
But only one little duck came back.

One little duck went out one day
Over the hills and far away.
Mother duck said, 'Quack quack, quack quack!'
But none of those five little ducks came back.

Mother duck she went out one day
Over the hills and far away.
Mother duck said, 'Quack quack, quack quack!'
And all of those five little ducks came back.

MARY HAD A LITTLE LAMB

Mary had a little lamb,
Its fleece was white as snow;
And everywhere that Mary went
The lamb was sure to go.

It followed her to school one day,
Which was against the rule;
It made the children laugh and play
To see a lamb at school.

And so the teacher turned it out,
But still it lingered near,
And waited patiently about
Till Mary did appear.

'What makes the lamb love Mary so?'
The eager children cry;
'Why, Mary loves the lamb, you know,'
The teacher did reply.

THE ANIMALS WENT IN TWO BY TWO

The animals went in two by two,
    Hurrah! Hurrah!
The animals went in two by two,
Hurrah! Hurrah!
The animals went in two by two,
The elephant and the kangaroo.
And they all went into the ark
For to get out of the rain.

The animals went in three by three
Hurrah! Hurrah!
The animals went in three by three,
Hurrah! Hurrah!
The animals went in three by three,
The wasp, the ant and the bumblebee.
And they all went into the ark
For to get out of the rain.

The animals went in four by four,
Hurrah! Hurrah!
The animals went in four by four,
Hurrah! Hurrah!

The animals went in four by four,
The great hippopotamus
    stuck in the door.
And they all went into the ark
For to get out of the rain.

The animals went in five by five,
Hurrah! Hurrah!
The animals went in five by five,
Hurrah! Hurrah!
The animals went in five by five,
They felt so happy to be alive.
And they all went into the ark
For to get out of the rain.

The animals went in six by six,
Hurrah! Hurrah!
The animals went in six by six,
Hurrah! Hurrah!
The animals went in six by six,
They turned out the monkey
    because of his tricks.
And they all went into the ark
For to get out of the rain.

The animals went in seven by seven,
Hurrah! Hurrah!
The animals went in seven by seven,
Hurrah! Hurrah!
The animals went in seven by seven,
The little pig thought he was going
   to heaven.
And they all went into the ark
For to get out of the rain.

The animals went in eight by eight,
Hurrah! Hurrah!
The animals went in eight by eight,
Hurrah! Hurrah!
The animals went in eight by eight,
The slithery snake slid under the gate.
And they all went into the ark
For to get out of the rain.

The animals went in nine by nine,
Hurrah! Hurrah!
The animals went in nine by nine,
Hurrah! Hurrah!

The animals went in nine by nine,
The rhino stood on the porcupine.
And they all went into the ark
For to get out of the rain.

The animals went in ten by ten,
Hurrah! Hurrah!
The animals went in ten by ten,
Hurrah! Hurrah!
The animals went in ten by ten,
And Noah said, 'Let's start again!'
And they all went into the ark
For to get out of the rain.

THREE LITTLE KITTENS

Three little kittens, they lost their mittens,
   And they began to cry;
Oh, mother dear, we sadly fear
That we have lost our mittens.
What! Lost your mittens, you naughty kittens!
Then you shall have no pie.
Mee-ow, mee-ow, mee-ow,
No, you shall have no pie.

Three little kittens, they found their mittens,
And they began to cry;
Oh, mother dear, see here, see here,
For we have found our mittens.
Put on your mittens, you silly kittens,
And you shall have some pie.
Purr-r, purr-r, purr-r,
Oh, let us have some pie.

Three little kittens put on their mittens,
And soon ate up the pie;
Oh, mother dear, we greatly fear
That we have soiled our mittens.
What! Soiled your mittens, you naughty kittens!
Then they began to sigh,
Mee-ow, mee-ow, mee-ow,
Then they began to sigh.

The three little kittens, they washed their mittens,
And hung them out to dry;
Oh, mother dear, do you not hear
That we have washed our mittens?
What! Washed your mittens, you good little kittens,
But I smell a rat close by.
Mee-ow, mee-ow, mee-ow,
We smell a rat close by.

SIX LITTLE MICE

Six little mice sat down to spin,
Pussy passed by, and she peeped in.
What are you doing, my little men?
Weaving coats for gentlemen.
Shall I come in and cut off your threads?
No, no, Mistress Pussy, you'd bite off our heads!
Oh, no, I won't, I'll help you to spin.
That may be so, but you can't come in!

The Wolf and the Seven Little Kids

There was once a goat who had Seven Little Kids. She loved them all, just as much as any mother loves her children. One day, she had to go into the woods to get some food for them all.

The Mother goat called all her children to her and told them, 'Dear children, I have to go into the woods. Now, do not open the door while I am away. You must be on guard for the Wolf. If he gets in, he will eat all of you up, and not even a hair would be left. The Wolf often tries to disguise himself, but you will recognise him at once by his rough voice and his black feet.'

'Mother dear, we will be very careful not to let the old Wolf in!' the Seven Little Kids cried. 'There is no need to worry about us.' So the Mother goat bleated and went on her way with her mind at ease.

It was not long before there was a loud knock at the door and a voice cried out, 'Open the door, my dear children! It is your Mother and I have brought something back for each of you.'

But the Little Kids knew from the rough voice that it was the Wolf at the door.

'We will not open the door!' they called out. 'You are not our Mother! Our Mother's voice is soft and gentle. Your voice is rough and hard. You are a Wolf!'

The old Wolf ran to a shop and bought himself a large piece of chalk, which he ate to make his voice soft, twisting his face up at the nasty taste. Then he went back and knocked at the door, calling out in his soft voice, 'Open the door, dear children! It is your Mother and I have brought something back for each of you.'

But the Wolf had laid one of his black paws on the window sill. The Seven Little Kids saw it and cried out, 'We will not open the door! You are not our Mother! Our Mother's feet are white. Yours are black. You are a Wolf!'

The old Wolf ran to the baker and said to him, 'Mr Baker, put some dough on my foot, for I have sprained it.'

After the baker had rubbed dough on his foot, the Wolf went to the miller and said, 'Sprinkle some white flour on my foot.'

The miller thought to himself, 'The Wolf wants to trick someone,' and refused to do it. But the Wolf said, 'If you will not do it, I will eat you up.' That frightened the miller, so he did as the Wolf asked and sprinkled white flour on his paw.

Then the Wolf went back to the goat's house and knocked on the door. He called out in his soft voice, 'Open the door, dear children! It is your Mother.'

The Seven Little Kids cried out, 'First, show us your foot!' So the Wolf put his one white foot on the window sill. When the Seven Little Kids saw that the foot was white, they thought it must be their Mother and opened the door. But no! It was the Wolf!

All the Little Kids ran to hide themselves. The first hid under the table, the second in the bed, the third in the oven, the fourth in the kitchen, the fifth in the cupboard, the sixth under the washbasin and the seventh, who was the smallest of all, in the grandfather clock. The Wolf quickly found them and gobbled them up. However, he did not find the youngest kid, who was in the clock.

After he had satisfied his appetite, the Wolf felt very sleepy. He went outside and found some green grass under a tree in the meadow. He lay down and went to sleep.

167

A little later, the Mother goat came back from the woods. The door was wide open, the tables and chairs were turned over, the washing bowl lay broken in pieces and the bedding had been torn off the bed. She looked for her children but none were to be seen. She called them by name, one after the other, but there was no answer until she came to the youngest. Then a soft voice cried out, 'Mother dear, I am hiding in the clock!'

The Mother goat rescued the youngest kid from the clock and learned how the Wolf had eaten her dear children. She went outside and saw the Wolf in the meadow, fast asleep on the grass. As the goat looked at the Wolf, she saw that his belly was jumping and jiggling.

'Goodness!' she thought. 'Is it possible that my poor children are still alive?'

The Mother goat sent the youngest kid inside to get a pair of scissors and a needle and thread. She quickly cut a hole in the Wolf's belly. At the first snip of the scissors, one of the kids stuck its head out of the hole. She cut a little more and one after the other, all six jumped out. They had suffered no injury whatsoever! They hugged their Mother and jumped about on the grass.

The Mother goat said, 'Quick, go and look for some big stones from the stream!'

The Seven Little Kids ran off to the stream and soon came back with seven large stones. They put the stones in the Wolf's belly and the Mother goat sewed the Wolf up so gently and quietly that he did not wake up or move.

At last the Wolf woke, feeling very thirsty. He stood up and the stones in his belly began to rattle and bump against each other. He walked slowly to the stream to drink, but when he bent over, the stones were so heavy that they tipped him over into the deep water. He sank without a trace and the Seven Little Kids danced for joy, singing, 'The Wolf is gone! The Wolf is gone!' The Mother goat hugged her Seven Little Kids and they all lived happily, and safely, ever after.

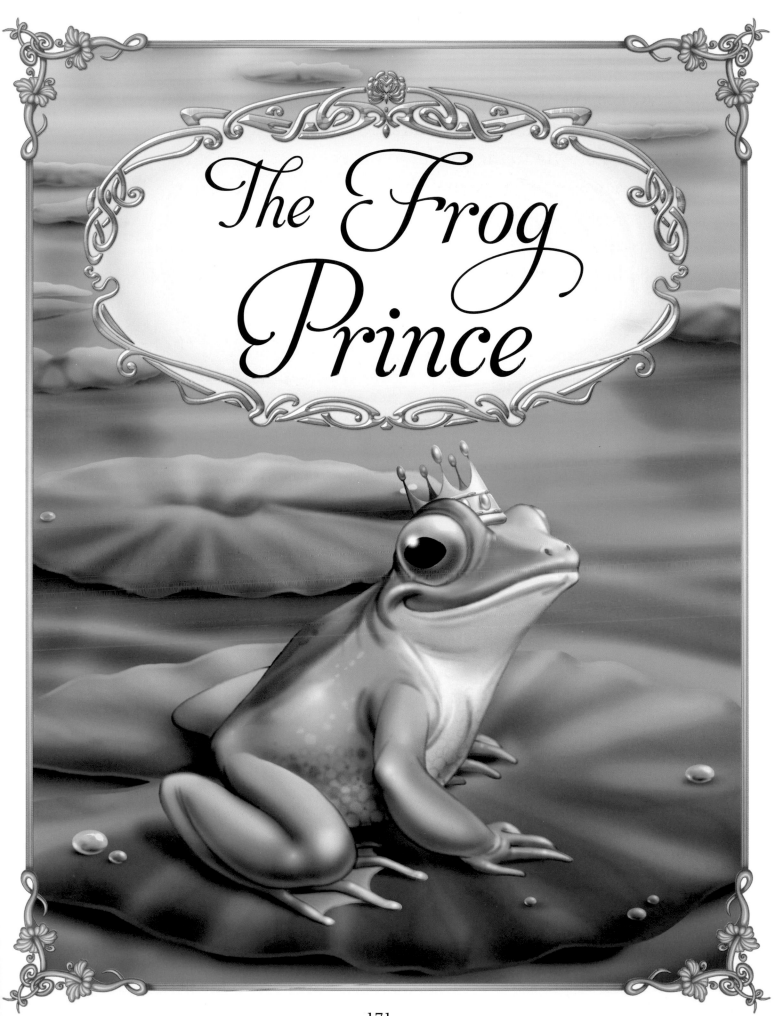

The Frog Prince

Once upon a time, there lived a king. His daughters were all beautiful, but the youngest was the most beautiful of all. A great forest lay next to the king's castle and in that forest was a deep well. On hot days, the youngest daughter would go to the forest and sit under a tree next to the well to play in the cool shade. The young princess's favourite plaything was a lovely golden ball, and there she would sit, tossing her ball in the air and catching it.

Alas, one day as she was sitting by the well, the princess threw her golden ball so high that instead of falling into her outstretched hand, it bounced away and rolled across the grass into the depths of the well. The princess ran to the side of the well, but she looked for her ball in vain, as the well was so deep that no one could see the bottom. The young princess began to weep at the loss of her favourite toy and could find no comfort.

As she sat crying, the young princess heard someone call out to her. 'Why do you weep so, princess?' said the voice. 'You cry so hard that you would even break the heart of a stone.'

The princess looked up to see where the voice was coming from and saw that a frog had lifted his ugly head out of the well and was talking to her.

'Alas, nasty frog,' she replied, 'I am weeping for my lovely golden ball. It has fallen into the well and is lost. Oh, what I would give to get it back!'

'Do not cry princess,' replied the slimy frog. 'I can help you, but what would you give me if I bring your ball back to you?'

'Whatever you ask for, dear frog,' said the princess. 'I would give all my fine clothes, my jewels, my pearls and even the precious golden crown on my head if I could get my ball back!'

'I care not for fine clothes, jewels, pearls or golden crowns,' answered the frog. 'But if you will love me and let me be your friend and playmate, and sit by you at your little table, and eat off your golden plate and drink out of your golden cup, and sleep on your pillow in your bed – if you will promise me this – then I will bring you back your golden ball from the depths of the well.'

'Oh yes!' cried the princess. 'If you will bring me my ball back, I promise I will do all you ask!'

But the princess was really thinking, 'How silly this frog is! All he can do is sit in the well with the other frogs and croak all day long. He's not fit to be anybody's playmate!'

So the frog dived down deep into the well. After a while, he swam back up to the surface again, holding the princess's golden ball in his mouth. He threw the ball over the edge of the well on to the grass and the princess ran and joyfully picked it up.

The princess was so happy to have her ball back that she ran away merrily, giving no thought to the frog and her promise.

'Wait princess! Don't forget your promise!' cried the frog. 'Take me with you! I cannot run as fast as you!'

But the princess did not hear the cries of the frog as she ran home to the castle. The poor frog was left to dive sadly back into the well.

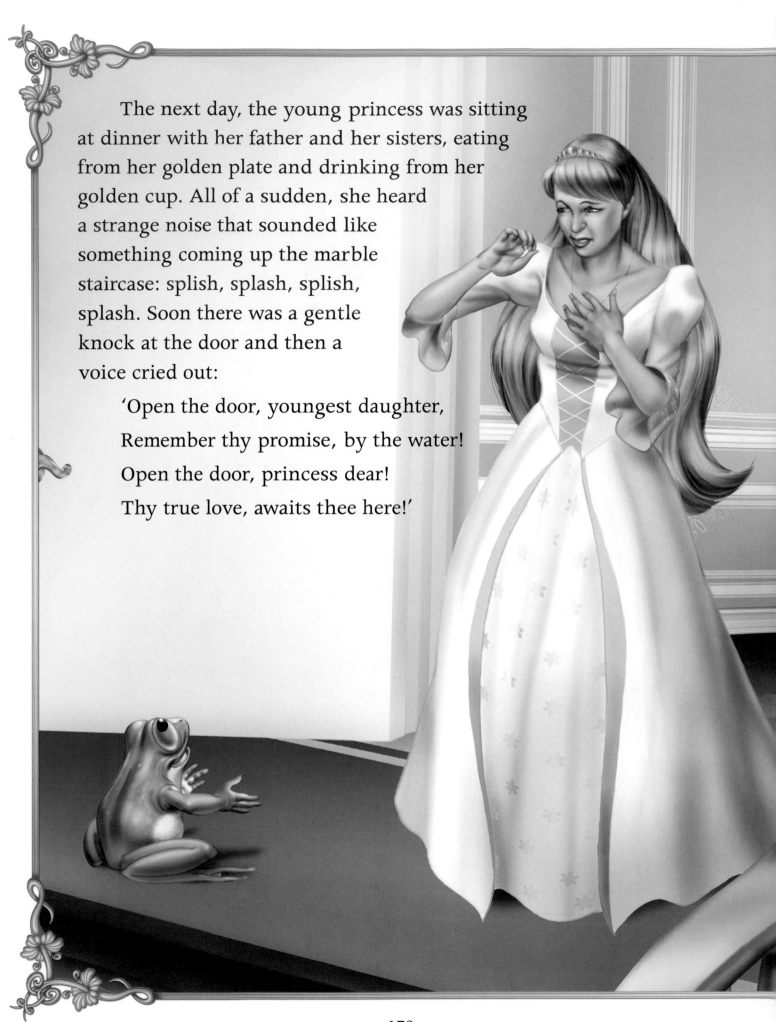

The next day, the young princess was sitting
at dinner with her father and her sisters, eating
from her golden plate and drinking from her
golden cup. All of a sudden, she heard
a strange noise that sounded like
something coming up the marble
staircase: splish, splash, splish,
splash. Soon there was a gentle
knock at the door and then a
voice cried out:

'Open the door, youngest daughter,
Remember thy promise, by the water!
Open the door, princess dear!
Thy true love, awaits thee here!'

The princess ran to the door to see who was there, but when she opened it, she saw the frog from the well sitting there. She slammed the door in fright and ran back to the table.

However, her father saw that something had frightened her and so he asked her, 'What ails you my daughter? Has some beast come to carry you away?'

'It is no beast, father,' the young princess explained. 'It is nothing but an ugly frog.'

'A frog?' asked the surprised king. 'What does a frog want with you?'

'Yesterday I was playing with my golden ball near the well,' the princess replied. 'It fell in the water and I couldn't get it out because the well is so deep. However, this frog fetched it for me after I promised that he could be my companion. I never thought he would leave the well, but here he is at the door, knocking to come in.'

180

Again there was a knock at the door, and again the frog cried out:

'Open the door, youngest daughter,

Remember thy promise, by the water!

Open the door, princess dear!

Thy true love, awaits thee here!'

The king turned to his daughter and said, 'As you have given your promise, you must keep your word. Do not refuse to help someone who has helped you. Go and let the frog in.'

So the princess opened the door and let the frog in. He hopped along behind her, following her back to her place at the table.

'Lift me up so I may eat off your golden plate and drink out of your golden cup!' the frog cried.

The princess tried to resist, but her father commanded her to keep her promise. 'You must keep your promise, daughter,' said the king.

So the princess lifted the frog up on to the table, where he ate from her golden plate and sipped from her golden cup. The frog ate well, but the princess hardly touched a morsel, so disgusted and upset was she.

Then the frog said, 'Now princess, I am tired. Carry me upstairs to your room and let me sleep next to you in your bed.'

The princess began to cry, as she hated the thought of the nasty frog asleep in her pretty silk sheets, but her father looked at her angrily and again said, 'As you have given your promise, you must keep your word. Do not forget your pledge. Remember, he helped you when you were in trouble.'

So the young princess carried the frog upstairs to her bedroom and laid him on her pillow, where he slept all night. As soon as the sun rose, the frog hopped downstairs and went back to the well.

'At last he is gone,' thought the relieved princess, 'and I shall hear from him no more.'

But the next evening as she was sitting down to dinner, the young princess again heard a gentle knock at the door and a voice crying out:

'Open the door, youngest daughter,

Remember thy promise, by the water!

Open the door, princess dear!

Thy true love, awaits thee here!'

Reluctantly, the princess let the frog dine with her and let him sleep on her pillow.

But she was becoming used to him now, and didn't find him quite so disgusting. After all, he was a polite frog, with good manners and lovely kind eyes. Again at sunrise, the frog hopped downstairs back to the well, and the princess found she actually missed his company.

The princess was not surprised to hear another knock at the door on the third night and a voice crying out:

'Open the door, youngest daughter,

Remember thy promise, by the water!

Open the door, princess dear!

Thy true love, awaits thee here!'

Again she dined with the frog, this time quite happily. She cheerfully chatted with him as they ate and carried him up to her room where again he slept on her pillow.

Imagine her surprise the next morning as the sun was rising when she woke. The princess was astonished to see, instead of a frog, a handsome prince standing next to her bed looking down on her with kind and beautiful eyes.

The handsome prince told her that he had been cursed by an evil witch, who had changed him into a frog. He was destined to stay a frog forever, unless a beautiful princess would let him eat from her plate and sleep on her pillow for three nights in a row.

'You have broken the evil spell,' the handsome prince said. 'Come with me to my father's kingdom and marry me and I will love you as long as you live.'

The young princess was overjoyed and accepted his hand in marriage.

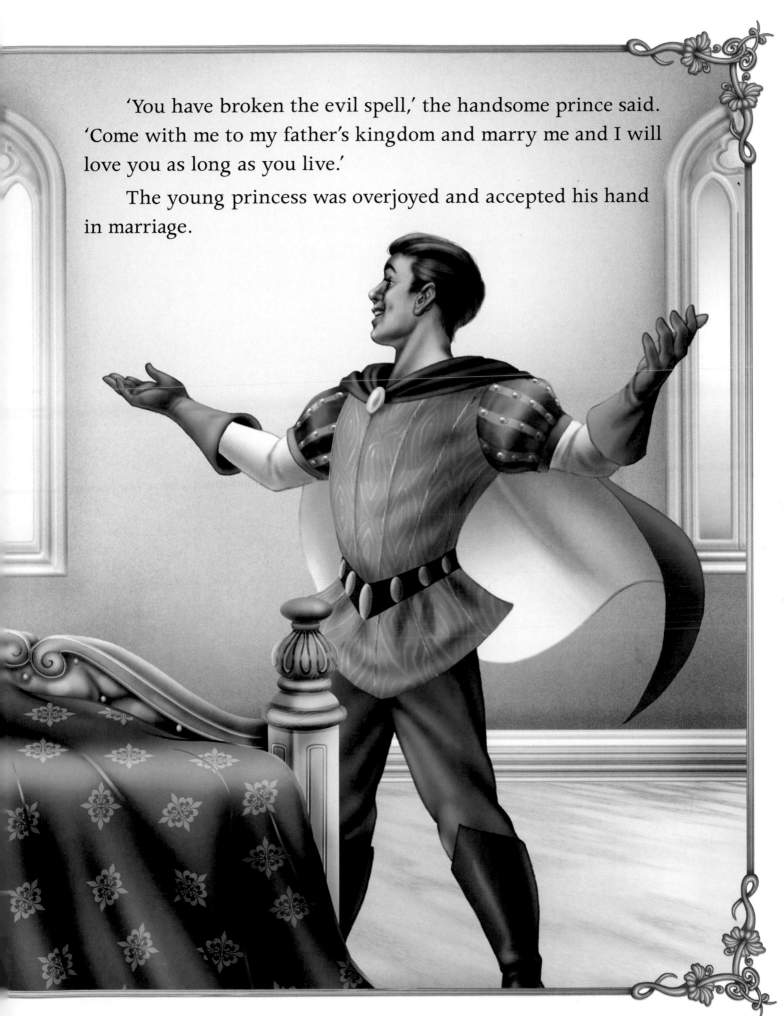

As they spoke together, a golden carriage drove up outside, pulled by eight powerful horses decked with feathers and a golden harness. Behind the coach was the prince's servant Faithful Henry, who had been so unhappy when his dear master had been turned into a frog by the witch that his heart had nearly broken.

Faithful Henry helped the prince and princess into the carriage and drove them to the prince's kingdom.

As they drove away, they heard the sound of Faithful Henry singing at the top of his voice, so overjoyed was he that his master was free and happy. When they reached the kingdom, the prince and the princess were married and lived happily ever after.